THE PONY SWAP

THE PONY SWAP

Pamela Kavanagh

Allen Junior Fiction

Published in Great Britain in 1994 by
J A Allen & Co. Ltd.
1 Lower Grosvenor Place
London SW1W 0EL

British Library Cataloguing in Publication Data
A catalogue record for this book is available
from the British Library

ISBN 0851316050

Jacket design by Nancy Lawrence
Jacket illustration by Jennifer Bell

ONE

"Whoa Comet! Oh, DO behave!" cried Nicky, battling with her new chestnut pony as he sidled dangerously close to the low branches of the trees. "Stop acting stupid. Oh, do walk on!"

Impatiently Nicky urged the chestnut back on to the path. This time it was a rabbit, scuttling from the bank, that had startled him. Yesterday it had been a bird in the hedge. Anything seemed to trigger him off. Nicky could not understand him.

Comet was still snorting and rolling his eyes, as if he expected more horrors to be lurking in the grass. Alarmed, Nicky did her best to sooth him, patting his shoulder and clicking her tongue. But when his tail gave that sudden warning flick she knew that it was hopeless and she stiffened in the smart new saddle. Sure enough, the pony's muscles bunched and, with a sideways plunge that almost unseated her, he began to play up.

Nicky fought him desperately, shouting, yanking on the reins, but Comet's mind was set. Ears flattened and tail lashing, he gave a small swift rear and launched himself into an explosive fly-buck, hurling Nicky on to his neck. Completely out of control now he shot forward, bucked again. . . and flung her neatly into the undergrowth.

Free at last, the chestnut galloped off, reins flying, hooves hammering the forest path.

Nicky had landed with a breath-grabbing thud amongst a rank growth of bracken and leafy hawthorn. Gasping, spluttering, she grabbed a branch and tried to pull herself up, but a hateful booming came to her ears and everything swam around her.

Mum'll go spare if Comet's lost, was her last thought as the trees slid away and blackness closed in.

"C'MON, SHAKE YOURSELF! THIS AIN'T NO PLACE TO TAKE A KIP!"

Jerked out of softly reeling darkness, Nicky groaned. She wished that whoever was speaking would go away. It was actually quite comfortable here on the ground, apart from the grass tickling her chin and, of course, that annoying voice. She felt the splash of water, ice-cold on her face. It was raining, she thought. She'd no coat. Still, just a few minutes. . .

A second torrent gushed, bringing her abruptly to her senses.

"Woke up at last?" came the voice again. "How d'you feel?"

Nicky's eyes struggled to focus. A boy, gypsy-dark, with piercing blue eyes and a lot of wild black hair, was kneeling beside her, water dripping from his hands. His look was anxious. "You ain't broke nothing," he assured. "You're just shocked. Try and breath deep. C'mon, in out, in out. . ."

Coughing a little Nicky responded. The boy's swarthy face split into an immediate grin, showing very white crooked teeth. "That's more like it! I were gettin' quite concerned. C'mon, let's sit you where you can rest a bit."

Nicky found herself hauled up out of the prickly grass and dumped down with her back to the bowl of a tree. She sat muzzily, her hair and shirt clinging, uncomfortably wet.

"Lucky the stream were close or you'd still be out cold!" the boy exclaimed, stooping with agile grace to dry his hands in the grass. He was still grinning, those incredibly blue eyes never leaving her face. "Winded real bad, you was. Hurts, don't it?"

Nicky nodded. Gingerly she flexed her arms and legs and wriggled her fingers. Everything seemed to be working and the fogginess was beginning to clear. Behind her eyes though was an ominous thrumming that was the start of one of her headaches. Pain, with the threat of more pain to come.

Easing off her tight headgear, Nicky leaned back and regarded the boy dully. Standing legs straddled, thumbs thrust into the back pockets of his shabby jeans, he looked full of wiry strength and vitality. His shirt was stained, his denim-jacket torn and grubby. In contrast, his short black-leather boots were immaculately polished to a high, hard gloss.

"Give me one heck of a fright you did, slumped in the grass like you was dead!" he said in his loud, flat voice. "Who the heck ARE you, anyway?"

Nicky cleared her throat. "N. . . Nicolette McGuire," she told him shakily. "Nicky to my friends—not that

I've made any yet. We've only been here a couple of months."

The boy snapped his fingers. "Now I place you! Come to The Briars, ain't you? Done the old place up real fancy."

"That's right." Nicky's tone was glum. White-walled and gabled, The Briars was her mother's dream home, its ample stabling and grassy paddocks affording much scope for a horsy family. Only they were not horsy. Dad scarcely knew one end of a pony from the other and she, Nicky, preferred drawing horses to riding them. It was just Mum, taking it into her head that competitive riding was the Thing To Do when you came to live in a place like Chantley.

Their new home, a mile or so up a winding lane from Chantley village, was surrounded by fields and overlooked the Wyre Forest.

"Nice spot," said the boy. "We're neighbours, sort of. You must'ave rode past the track to Keeper's Lodge when you come to the forest?" Nicky's stare was absent and his thin shoulders lifted in a shrug. "That's our place anyway. Me name's Zackery Shone—er, Zak to me friends!" The grin was back, direct and mocking.

Nicky shifted about uneasily on the hard ground. She really should make a move to go, but the fall had left her distinctly wobbly, her chest sore, her head pounding, and it was easier just to sit.

But Mum might be getting anxious, an inner voice reminded. Comet was not usually kept out so long. And then it occurred to her. Where WAS the chestnut?

"COMET!" she blurted. "Oh heck, I bet the beastly creature's in the next county by now! Mum'll be furious.

Oh heck, where is he?"

Zak opened his mouth to speak but in blind panic Nicky had pulled herself up and was stumbling to the edge of the path. She glanced wildly up and down, listening, her ears straining. No sign of Comet, not even a hint of hoofbeat. Nothing but tall trees casting their silent shadows.

A tap on her shoulder brought her wheeling round. Zak had followed and was regarding her in total perplexity. "You do tear yourself up rather, don't you?" he said. "I keep trying to tell you, I've caught your 'oss, no problem!"

He crooked a grimy thumb and there, almost hidden behind a screen of leafy hawthorn, stood a sweaty and subdued Comet. He was still blowing slightly and his tail flicked impatiently at the flies.

"O . .oh!" Through Nicky's obvious relief came that familiar stab of irritation that Comet was inclined to provoke. She gave Zak a tight smile. "Thanks a lot. Mum would go SPARE if anything happened to him."

"Think nothing of it," said Zak. "He's broke a rein, but that ain't much, considerin' the way he was tearin' through the forest! Got himself in a proper spin. I loosed his girth an' ran up his stirrups. Want a hand with him?"

It was the understatement of the decade!

Together they made a move through lanky grass and clinging bracken towards the pony, but as they pushed into the thicket of summer hawthorn, Nicky stopped dead.

Not one, but two chestnuts were here. Rubbing her smarting eyes, Nicky stammered, "I. . .I must have double vision or something! My head DOES ache something chronic but—"

"T'other's my Cobber," Zak confirmed with a chuckle.

"Huh, I might have guessed you were on a pony!" Nicky retorted, shooting Zak's boots a disdainful glance.

The polished heels clicked together smartly. "I don't care what sorta kit I wear," Zak declared, as if it were of the utmost importance. "But I got to have the right footgear else I feel all wrong on an 'oss."

Nicky, who could not wait to get her own jod boots off and her feet into something blissfully unhorsy, frowned across at the two ponies. Their resemblance was uncanny. Height, build, right down to their rich red-gold colour made it difficult, in the wavering light of the forest, to tell them apart.

Comet was now pulling at his tether. The other stood free, rock-still, his reins dangling like a cow pony's. Edging closer, Nicky now saw that he had a white blaze on his face and his near fore sported a white sock, otherwise—.

"Spitting image, ain't they?" Zak echoed her thoughts exactly. "Difference is my Cobber's well schooled. He don't go tearin' down the trails like he was trainin' for the National!"

He laughed, and getting no response from Nicky, put his fingers to his mouth and gave a piercing whistle. The little chestnut came over promptly, walking with careful steps to stop, like a well-disciplined dog, beside his owner. Zak ruffled the bushy mane fondly. "See what I mean?"

Nicky was scrabbling for a suitable answer when Comet, finding himself ignored, gave a fraught little whinny and began to paw the ground. Nicky had just about had enough. "Oh give over, you stupid beast!" she cried. "You've done enough harm for one day!"

Zak's face tightened. Without a word he went across to Comet, striding with springy precision over the grass. A swift jerk released the tether and Zak led the chestnut back. Nicky took Comet reluctantly, her heart sinking when she saw the expensive leather rein, snapped near the buckle.

"Oh heck, Mum'll scalp me over this," she groaned. "It's new tack and she's for ever on at me to clean it, and to hang it up properly, and dry it if it gets wet—"

"Sounds a real pain, your ma!" Zak commented lightly. "Reckon she's right all the same. You got to look after leather or it goes rotten an' cracks."

He grinned again. Nicky scowled. His teeth reminded her of a terrier's they had once had, all snaggled but right for the job.

Pulling a filthy rag that might have begun life as a handkerchief from his pocket, Zak briskly rubbed the whitish crusting of dried sweat from Comet's neck and flanks. This done, he stood back, head tilted, and flicked a speculative eye over the pony. "Not bad. Not bad at all. In fact he's quite a good little' oss—"

"You've got to be joking!" Nicky spluttered. "Comet's an absolute horror! He's virtually unmanageable. Nothing on this earth would convince me that he's GOOD!"

Her voice rose shrilly but Zak, still lost in admiration for the pony, simply stood and stared, ignoring her completely.

Fighting tears of annoyance and frustration, coupled

with the sneaking knowledge that Comet's behaviour was very likely due to her own incapacity to control him, Nicky lurched forward and before she could stop herself, had fetched the pony a furious, unworthy lash across his neck with the broken rein.

Comet flinched and rolled a wary eye, and Zak sprang to calm him. He then turned on Nicky reproachfully. "Aye, you shouldn't do that!" he chided, his face frowning and indignant. "The poor little 'oss don't like it."

"Comet doesn't like anything, me least of all!" Nicky winced as a fresh pain exploded inside her head. "If he's not trying to throw me he's rearing, or tearing off. He's a PIG and I absolutely HATE him!"

"Then why 'd you get him?"

"I didn't!" said Nicky. "It was Mum, insisting I had a good pony."

"Like I said"—Zak scowled—"sounds a real pain, your ma!"

Mutely Nicky shook her head. Her anger had gone but the tears were still there, unshed, stinging her eyes. Blinking them back, she dropped her gaze and kicked dejectedly at the dusty path. Everything had been fine until Dad had landed his new job and they had moved to Chantley. Her parents, of course, were thrilled at their improved lifestyle. Dad's new job offered many perks; big car, better house, new clothes for Mum.

And for herself there was Comet.

Nicky pulled a face. Worst of all though, was the way Mum had changed. She used to be a funloving person, busy with her Meals On Wheels and her PTA, whose idea of relaxation was a brisk walk over the fell. Now, all that interested her was turning the house into a showplace and buying showy gear for the pony. The difference in her was hardly credible, and each morning Nicky clattered downstairs hoping that Mum would be back to normal. Unfortunately this had not happened. She was beginning to doubt it ever would.

"Where 'd you get that little 'oss?"

"What's that?" Nicky surfaced to meet Zak's intent stare. Stamping the earth back into the hole she had dug in the Forest floor, she gave a shrug. "Oh, Comet came from a dealer's yard, near where we used to live."

"Where was that?"

"Up north," Nicky said wistfully. "We had a cottage in the fells with a sort of straggly orchard and a stable. Dad worked for the tourist board in Appleby. . ." Her old home rose sharply in her mind. She could almost smell the wind, fresh off the sea and tasting of salt. Different from Shropshire, with its rolling pastures and wooded valleys.

"Appleby, aye?" Zak's eyes had taken on a gleam. "D'you ever see the Horse Fair?"

Nicky shook her head disgustedly. "It was too rough. People getting drunk and fighting. Mum wouldn't go near."

Zak gave a rich chuckle and Comet lowered his head and nudged him playfully in the stomach. With a gentle hand Zak pushed him away, but the chestnut only edged closer and began to lip the boy's palm.

Nicky was aghast. "Comet NEVER does that to me. He's just a pain all the time."

"That's because you don't handle him right." Zak treated Comet to a hearty slap on the neck. "I reckon your Comet'll be a cracking little 'oss, once you master him."

Some hope! thought Nicky, darting a wary glance. But Zak was now frowning at Comet's bridle with its kimblewick and curb chain, which was badly twisted. His nimble fingers set to work at once, straightening the chain so that it lay flat and comfortable under the pony's chin.

"It's no wonder the 'oss chucked you an' ran," he said. "He were only trying to get away from that. It hurt him. see? An' another thing, a kimblewick should have a leather strap under the chain—"

"It was like that when we got it," Nicky cut in sulkily. "No one ever mentioned curb straps or anything else."

"Well they should've!" Zak persisted, his lip curling. "Don't hold with them fancy gadgets anyway. 'Oss'd go better in a snaffle."

"But I'd never manage him," Nicky said. "I couldn't even stop him in that wretched kimblewick thing!"

"Like I said—'

"I HEARD!" Nicky affected a bored sigh and said mockingly, "The poor dear little pony was running away from his poor hurting mouth! Huh I should care!" Her voice wobbled. "He almost killed me, and it wasn't the first time. He's ALWAYS up to tricks! How I'm going to jump him this season I can't imagine!"

A crafty glimmer was sneaking into Zak's eyes but he said, quite sympathetically, "I reckon Comet's too keen for you. A first pony should be real quiet, to give you confidence like."

"Comet's my second," Nicky said swiftly. "Fella was great. Dead slow, more my sort."

Zak was not listening. Whistling tunelessly he began

to examine the chestnut, first glancing into his mouth and then circling him, lifting the long tail, fingering the glossy mane. He ran a hand down Comet's clean legs and inspected each neat hoof. To Nicky's astonishment Comet lifted his feet without protest, a thing he had never done for her. She had not cleaned them out in ages for that very reason. Finally Zak gave the muscled quarters a resounding slap. He turned to Nicky.

"You say he jumps?" The question was put casually, but Zak's eyes were glinting.

There and then, Nicky should have been suspicious. Instead she answered him openly. "Of course he jumps. That's why Mum bought him. He's SUPPOSED to be a schoolmaster. He's eight."

"Fourish!" Zak corrected promptly. Nicky stared in dismay, but when she began to bewail the fact Zak admonished her soundly for not checking.

"I can't tell by a horse's teeth anyhow," she muttered. "And Mum didn't look. She just took the dealer's word."

"I dunno!" Zak shook his head pityingly. "I reckon that guy sure saw you coming!"

There was a deep silence. The forest murmured around them, secretive little rustlings and stirrings. Nicky shuddered. She had not taken to Chantley, there was something sinister about the place. She missed her friends as well. With Fella sold she did not even enjoy her riding, and now she was lumbered with this half-wild pony that was supposed to bring her success in the jumping ring. Unhappily she fingered the broken rein.

"Can mend that, if you want," Zak offered.

Nicky jerked up. At least it would save any trouble from Mum. "Could you really?" she said. "That would be great!"

Zak's expression was now guileless. "One rein'll be a mite short, otherwise you'll never spot the difference," he promised moving to tighten Cobber's girth. Those glittering eyes still watched, levelly, not missing a thing. Nicky found their stare quite disconcerting.

"How come you know how to repair tack?" she asked.

"I do anything round 'osses," Zak said matter-of-factly. "Buy 'em, break 'em, AND I fix their gear. Got to, in my trade."

So he was a horse dealer. That explained it all.

Vaulting into the saddle, Zak shoved his booted toes in the stirrups and jerked his head towards Comet. "Get on then, Nick. Let's go!"

Slowly Nicky replaced her hat, wincing as it gripped her throbbing head. Her fingers fumbled to fasten the chin strap. Heart thumping, she tightened Comet's girth, pulled down the stirrups, and gathered the reins. Sensing her reluctance, Comet sidled restlessly. His head tossed, his eyes showed the whites. Nicky's mouth went dry.

"You getting on today or tommorra?" Zak was impatient. he nudged Cobber on to the path.

Nicky felt her stomach lurch. She backed off, shaking her head. "I'm not getting on him at all," she said miserably. "No way do I want to ride Comet ever again!"

TWO

It was a long walk back to Keeper's Lodge.

Nicky had expected Zak to scoff at her refusal to ride Comet, and she had scarcely believed her luck when he had merely shrugged and said blandly, "OK, Nick, we'll tramp. Cobber's tired, anyway." Slipping from Cobber's back, he had taken charge of both sets of reins and pointed the way.

They went in silence along the cool, green tunnels, the ponies plodding behind them. With her throbbing head and stiffening muscles, Nicky was beginning to regret her decision to go with Zak. All she wanted was to be home. She had intended getting Comet's exercise out of the way and then escaping to her room with her sketchbook and pencils.

Drawing was her passion, her release from the daily grind, and, more recently, from the trauma of being a new pupil in a good but demanding school. Stirring emotion went into her pencil strokes, feelings she endured, but could not understand. Now her plans were ruined, and all because of a no-good pony which she had never wanted in the first place.

Flies buzzed over the dusty path. Overhead the summer trees shivered their leaves, and faint stirrings in the undergrowth brought uneasy little snorts from Comet. Nicky's spirits sank lower with every step.

Zak turned to her suddenly. "You done much riding, Nick?"

Nicky shook her head. "Fella was more of a pet," she confessed. "But Mum's expecting me to compete on Comet, like she did when she was young. She's kept all her rosettes and we've lots of horsy photographs of people handing her trophies and her smiling." Nicky glanced sideways to find Zak still watching her.

"S'pose you've joined the Pony Club?" he said.

Nicky nodded gloomily. It was mid-July and the summer holidays stretched before her with a succession of rallies, culminating in a big event at the end of August: Chantley Horse Show and Gymkhana. She swallowed. The Chantley Branch of the Pony Club had a vast following and the very thought of all those ponies and riders, who came from miles around in swish wagons or trailers, triggered a feeling of panic. "I've already attended one rally, just to watch," she told Zak shakily. "I suppose it was all right. A bit boring. They spent ages walking round in circles."

"That's to teach you control," Zak said. "You should do what they tell you, then you'll manage your 'oss better!"

"I managed Fella well enough!" Nicky retorted. "I suppose you're a Pony Club member, too?"

Zak snorted. "You've got to be joking! I've more 'oss sense in me little finger than them instructors have between them! Besides, I don't take to being bossed by Ma Parks-Harrison!"

"Me neither!" agreed Nicky. Hearty and domineering, the District Commissioner of the Chantley Branch of the Pony Club had not made a favourable impression. "The way people bow and scrape to her makes me sick!"

"That's cos she's gentry!" Zak informed.

"Gentry?" Nicky sniggered. "That's a bit outdated, isn't it?"

"The Parks-Harrisons used to own Chantley, you know, so we all still think of them as gentry," Zak said. "Ma Parks-Harrison were forced to sell the land an' properties after her old man died. Couldn't keep the place going. Caused a deal o' bother."

"Oh?" Nicky stared curiously. "What sort of bother?"

Zak did not answer, and Nicky realized that he was frowning at the path ahead. He isn't even listening, she thought peevishly. Raising a hand to her throbbing temple, she tried again. "Have you always lived at Keeper's Lodge?"

Zak blinked. "What'd you say?"

Impatiently Nicky repeated her question and Zak told her in crushing tones of course he had, where else? "Then I suppose," Nicky soldiered on, "your father must be gamekeeper?"

This prompted a scowl, quick and fierce. "He WAS, before Parks-Harrison sold up. There ain't no keeper now, not since Nigel Gregory took over."

Nicky's interest quickened. "Dad works for Nigel Gregory," she said. "He manages the leisure parks. There are five of them. Nigel Gregory owns them all."

"Does he now!" Zak said, scathingly. "Well that don't

impress me one bit. We don't take kindly to business tycoons buying up our village."

"Why not?" Nicky asked, puzzled.

"Chantley's a mess since Gregory bought it, that's what!" Zak replied. "The man might be a whizz in the leisure game, but he ain't no countryman. What does he want with farmland, woods and heath? He's ruined the meadows, building himself a posh new house where a house never ought to be. And then. . ." Zak paused and flicked savagely at a pestering fly.

"And then what?" Nicky pressed.

Zak sent a smouldering blue glare. "Neglects the place, don't he? Country estates need MANAGING. They don't run themselves." He drew a quick breath. "Old Mr P-H now, he RULED Chantley."

"Ruled?" Nicky challenged. "That sounds positively feudal!"

"Well it weren't," Zak said. "Chantley were run proper. Now Ma Parks-Harrison's been left with just the Manor and a few piddling acres for the 'chasers."

"But I thought you didn't like the DC?" argued Nicky, who was beginning to think Zak the most contradictory character she had ever met.

"I never said that!" Zak cleared his throat noisily and spat in the bushes. "I said she were bossy, that don't mean I don't like her."

Nicky decided to change the subject. "So what does your dad do now?"

"How would I know?" Zak muttered. "Made off, ain't he? Not seen him in years."

Nicky's cheeks went pink and she began a stammered apology, but Zak shrugged her words aside. "It's OK,

Nick, me and me gran have shook in together fine. An' I've got me 'osses." A warmth crept into his voice and he smiled. "Got a nice place for 'osses yourself, ain't you, Nick?"

"I suppose so." Nicky sighed. "Mum's obsessed with doing the house up, though. It's all new this, new that. Mind the paint, don't breath on the antiques or tread mud on the carpets—"

"Well I dunno!" Zak gave his head a wry shake. "I'm that sorry for you I could holler!"

Nicky stiffened. She was about to make some acid response when she saw that Zak was grinning, his eyes crinkling merrily at the corners. With his hooked nose and tangled curls his face had a Puckish look, and despite herself Nicky giggled. At once Zak let out a hoot of laughter, so loud that Comet shied violently into the bushes.

It took Zak some minutes to steady the pony, with Nicky holding Cobber and looking on in exasperation. "Stupid beast!" she muttered, her good-humour disappearing. "Cobber wasn't a bit bothered."

"That's cos I trained him proper," Zak said smugly.

They set off again. The trees were now beginning to thin out. Sunshine lit the path in gentle golden shafts. Nicky smelt the tang of woodsmoke and heard, faintly, the busy clucking of hens.

"Almost there," Zak said, clicking his tongue to the ponies.

A frenzied barking marked their arrival at Keeper's Lodge. Handing the reins to Nicky, Zak went to untie the knotted string that secured the gate. The barking, which had come from inside the house, stopped. Nicky surveyed the hotchpotch yard of sheds and hutches and chicken cotes with dismay. A strong, animal smell pervaded the air, suggesting a great deal of livestock in too little space.

The lodge itself wore a neglected look, with its dingy walls and peeling paintwork. The narrow, pointed windows were smeared and dusty. Above the door a once impressive stone lintel, bearing the Chantley coat of arms of two rearing unicorns within a frame of ragged oak leaves, was cracked and crumbling. Decades of soot blackened the tall chimney, which billowed smoke in furious clouds.

Nicky's last shred of resolve crumbled. If only she'd gone home.

Her eye was then drawn to the flowering plants and feathery herbs that crowded the windowsills—somebody boasted very green fingers. As well, Zak's horse breaking evidently extended to driving, for inside the gate stood a scarlet-painted flatcart, its tail and headboard ornately scrolled in blue and black. The wheels were yellow, as was the narrow driving seat. It was jaunty and picturesque and Nicky had a compelling urge to draw it; with a gypsy pony in the shafts maybe, and a dark-faced tinker aboard, wielding a long whip.

Nicky looked closer at the row of sturdy sheds and pens. In one a grizzled old dogfox, hobbling with a foreleg in plaster met her astonished gaze. Another housed a white goat with a damaged horn. At the far end a spacious aviary held what looked like a variety of wild birds, some making hesitant flutters from one rustic perch to the next, others not.

"What's wrong with those sparrows?" Nicky questioned. But Zak, still intent upon the string, failed to answer.

Enclosing two sides of the yard was a low stable block, its thick stone walls set with cracked and filthy windows. At one end was a battered double door, and at the other a flight of uneven steps rose steeply to a feed loft. The pitching roof, lacking many slates, bore witness to countless winter gales.

Behind the stable loomed a Dutch barn, stuffed to the roof with hay. Cheerful hens pecked amongst the weedy cobblestones, and a steaming midden was the vantage point for the yard's cockerel who, seeing visitors, spread his jewelled wings and crowed with ear-splitting clamour. From a tangled orchard a couple of shaggy donkeys brayed forlornly.

The string yielded to Zak's fingers and, pushing open the gate, he gestured Nicky in. Nicky and Cobber came with eager strides but Comet, suspicious of the yard, typically refused to budge. "Come on, stupid!" Nicky hissed, giving the rein a jerk.

Zak rounded on her indignantly. "Not like that! Let him look, then coax him. Here, let me."

With an encouraging click of his tongue Zak took the rein and the pony gave in, allowing himself to be led between the cluttered buildings. Nicky, intrigued by the animals, followed more slowly with Cobber. On reaching the stable door Cobber stopped and assumed his stand, head down, ears slack.

"Drop the rein and he'll stay put as long as you like," Zak said, returning Comet to Nicky and going to battle with yet more string. Nicky considered that a few decent locks and bolts might be in order, but she was careful not to say so.

She scanned the pens. The first contained a red squirrel looking oddly lopsided due to a stitched ear. In the next several hedgehogs snoozed in a bed of straw. Then came rabbits, a couple of leggy hares, even a sharp-faced ferret. Further along, just visible above a corrugated metal barrier, poked an inquisitive grey and white snout.

"A badger!" Nicky gasped. "Oh, I've just GOT to go and look."

Zak had his back to her and made no reply, so dragging a reluctant Comet she went to peer into the cage.

It was a young badger, about half-grown. Not in the least afraid, it shuffled closer and reared up against the wire mesh, displaying a soft, whitish underbelly. Small, deep-set eyes regarded her inquisitively. Nicky was about to reach over and stroke it when there came a sudden warning shout.

Zak was at her side in a couple of bounds. "You got to watch badgers, Nick!" he cried. "Them can fetch a nasty bite!"

"Oh. . . I never thought." Nicky withdrew her hand reluctantly.

"He looks so tame, too. Is he a pet?"

"She!" Zak corrected. "She's damaged herself somehow. Me gran thinks another badger bit her. Sows tends to squabble, like a lot o' silly women. She's got a wound gone septic." He pointed out a hind leg, which was neatly bandaged from paw to stifle.

Nicky shot the row of pens a mystified glance. "Where do all these creatures come from?" she questioned. "Are they yours?"

"Heck no!" Zak was horrified. "They're me gran's.

Folk find 'em and dump 'em on her to heal. She's got a fawn here, too, but it was hurt real bad so she's kept it inside."

"Oh!" Nicky's eyes slid to the lodge.

"Me gran ain't in," Zak informed shrewdly. "She's caretaker at the school and she spring cleans in the holidays. Come back later. Happen she'll show you round."

Nicky looked entranced at the badger's dense, grey-flecked fur, her short bushy tail and fat-padded paws. Again she ached for her drawing materials. With Fella she had always carried them as he had stood whilst she sketched from his saddle. Comet of course, would not. Involuntarily she gave his rein a snatch.

All this time Comet's eyes had been popping at the badger. He was wary of the creature, which was making little grunting noises remarkably like a pig. Comet hated pigs. A little tremor shot through him. He squealed nervously and Nicky glanced up just in time to catch his tail, giving that warning flick.

"WATCH OUT!" she shouted in panic. "HE'S GOING TO REAR!"

Zak was at the pony's head instantly and Comet found himself jollied round in determined circles, a firm hand on his rein, a voice that was both commanding and reassuring in his ear. Each circle brought him a fraction closer to the badger, but when Zak finally halted him beside the creature, Comet still blew a gusty snort of disapproval.

Smoothing the ruffled forelock and looking the pony straight in the eye, the boy stood patiently for what seemed ages. Comet was distinctly puzzled, and then Zak began a strange, high-pitched whistling noise between his teeth. Comet's ears went back to the sound. The whistling continued, a long, pulsing note, hauntingly off-key. First soft, now building to an intense crescendo that buzzed and echoed even inside Nicky's head.

Just as the sound became almost too much to bear the tone softened again, falling in a gentle phrase that crept around the crowded yard and shivered to its conclusion.

All along the row of pens, the animals were silent, bright-eyed and watchful. They listened. Comet's ears flicked back and forth. Nicky saw his eyes lose that awful terror and take on a look of tranquillity. The frightened quivering ceased, and with a final shuddering sigh the pony stood, dazed and repentant, awaiting Zak's next word.

It came chidingly. "You daft thing! A right sweat you got yourself into over nothing!"

Comet all but purred! With a jangle of bit and curb chain he strained forward and lipped Zak's hand, and then he began to rake his head vigorously up and down Zak's body, showing his gratitude and establishing his trust.

Nicky could hardly believe it. For two whole months she had tried all ways to gain Comet's confidence and failed utterly. She watched as Zak produced a sliver of carrot from his pocket and fed it to the pony.

"That's spoiling him," he said, a touch shamefaced. "As a rule I don't hold with giving titbits, but that time, your little 'oss deserved it! Now take him an' follow us in. OK?"

He whistled up Cobber and they went from the sunlight into the dim, steamy warmth of the stable, where the sweet smell of hay and animals enfolded them. Zak chirruped a greeting and horses stamped and blew and flicked their tails in response.

The building was roughly sectioned into two long rows of stalls. These ended in a pair of roomy stallion boxes. Nicky's heart sank when she saw the central aisle, into which projected a great many well-muscled hindquarters. No way did she relish walking Comet between them. She stood, hanging grimly on to the pony's head, listening to the sound of Cobber's hooves clopping steadily away from her.

"You coming today or tomorra?" Zak called, leading the pony into the left-hand stallion box and beginning the business of untacking and rubbing down.

Drawing a determined breath, Nicky gave Comet's head a yank. He came in a rush, flinching and snorting, his hooves slithering on the well-trodden floor. Tails swished, straw rustled and heads turned enquiringly, eyes flashing a liquid gleam. Nicky dragged the chestnut past rumps pied and plain, dappled, spotted and flea-bitten. The final stall held a whiskered, coloured vanner with huge ears and a Roman nose, who raised a hairy hoof as they scuppered by. Gaining the empty stallion box, Nicky hurled Comet into it and slammed shut the door.

Now she had to untack.

It was a moment she had dreaded. She glanced over at Zak to see if he was watching, but he was grooming Cobber with long smooth strokes. As he worked, he whistled tunelessly. It was a sound all the horses seemed to enjoy, judging by their flicked ears and contented expressions.

Even Comet was listening, so summoning her last

thread of courage, Nicky entered the wide, straw-filled box. Comet eyed her warily. With tentative fingers Nicky ran up his stirrups and undid the girth, and sure enough, up came a threatening hoof. She was though, able to remove the saddle without further trouble, decided this could be due to Zak's soothing whistling, she approached Comet's head with a little more confidence than usual. Comet allowed her to unbuckle the throatlash, but when she unhooked the curb chain his ears flattened and his eyes went small and mean.

Nicky yanked off the bridle and dived for the door.

She made it just in time. Comet swung round with teeth bared, striking the frame with a resounding crash. Alarm shivered through the building. Chains rattled, hooves clattered and startled whinnies tore the air.

Zak was out of Cobber's box in a wink and skudding down the aisle. He moved like a shadow amongst the stamping horses, quick and graceful, calming each one with voice and hand until peace was eventually restored.

Nicky stood mutely, glowering at Comet over the door. She turned to find Zak, hands on hips, staring at her in sheer disbelief. "Does you 'oss always act up like that in his stable?" he asked acidly.

"Almost always," Nicky admitted.

Resting his bony elbows on the door Zak regarded the chestnut thoughtfully. Comet was pacing, pawing up straw. "Reckon he ain't really a bad lot," Zak said at last. "He's got a lot to learn and you're not teaching him right. He don't know where he stands."

"Comet NEVER stands!" Nicky cried. "He's a fidget!"

"That's cos you worry him. It's natural for an 'oss to

try and get away from what he don't like."

Receiving no reply, Zak went back to grooming his pony. Cobber stood relaxed, his lower lip drooping, his eyelids half-closed. Nicky's look was envious and Zak, noting this, gave the pony's neck an affectionate slap. "A real saint, is my Cobber," he said. "He's only one vice and that ain't nothing much."

"Oh really?" said Nicky with suspicion. "What does he do? Try to kill you when you go in his field?"

"Don't be daft!" Zak snapped. "I said it weren't much and it ain't. All he does wrong is pull back if you tether him. I've mended more halters since I got him than I'd like to count. Tried all ways to cure him—no go!" Zak gave one of his shrugs. "That's why I trained him to stand, see, like the cow ponies."

Nicky asked, "Have you had him long?"

"Few years, mebbe." Zak was evasive. "Other 'osses come an' go, but my Cobber sorta stays."

"Where did you get him from?"

"Can't remember, can I?" Zak said tetchily. "What a one you are for questions!"

Nicky heaved a sigh. Her head hurt abominably and the airless stable with its strong odour of horse suddenly got to her. She swayed, hand to her brow.

"You OK, Nick?"

"Head aches," she mumbled uncertainly. She also felt slightly sick. Zak fixed her with that hard stare and she braced herself for some caustic comment. It did not come.

"Bit a concussion mebbe," Zak said, quite kindly. "Got a cure for that, back in the house. I'd best deal with that rein, too."

Exchanging brush for a battered biscuit tin crammed to overflowing with tools and twines and old brass buckles, Zak gave his head a jerk. "Grab your bridle, let's go."

They went out again into the bright morning. Zak darted off to the house and Nicky settled herself on a straw bale with her back to the sunwarmed wall. it was somewhat fresher out here, and gulping lungfuls of air, she took stock of the situation.

Her hair and shirt were dry now. There was a telltale greenish path on her jods, but Mum was used to that. Just the rein to repair, then she could go. She glanced at her watch. Ten thirty. There might even be time to get in a couple of drawings before lunch, that is, if her headache didn't worsen. She badly wanted to capture that badger while it was clear in her mind.

"Here, Nick. Drink this." Zak was back, offering a measure of greenish-coloured syrup. Nicky eyed the concoction suspiciously. "It's what me gran brews from herbs an' such," Zak said, pressing the glass into her hand. "Won't do no harm, promise!"

That concentrated stare brooked no argument. Nicky raised the glass to her mouth and swallowed. The mint-flavoured syrup slid easily down her throat, making her insides comfortingly warm. Soon a languid feeling stole over her and she leaned back again, the sharpness still on her tongue.

Zak was removing the reins from Comet's bridle and cursing broadly over the stiffness of the new leather. Hunkering down, he rummaged in the tin for knife and needle and twine. Nicky watched him trim the jagged leather, and he was matching up the ends, prior to stitching, when she realized that her headache was lessening.

The relief was immense but she was puzzled. Mum had spent a fortune at the chemist, trying this painkiller and that, and nothing had worked. She turned grateful eyes on Zak.

"Told you!" was all he said. He began to sew with deft, even stitches, a frown of fierce concentration on his face. At intervals he darted a quick little glance, as though he expected her to speak. Nicky guessed at his age. Fifteen, maybe. Young, to be running a dealer's yard single-handed.

"Don't you go to school?" she asked curiously.

Zak threw a grin. "Not if I can help it! They don't learn you about 'osses at school. Besides"—his lip curled—"I never was popular with teachers. S'pose you're at Chantley village?"

Nicky shook her head.

"Comprehensive?"

"I'm only ten. I go to Mountbank, actually. It's not bad, but I'd prefer the village. You make more friends that way."

"Tall, ain't you, for ten?" Zak observed. "Good thing I've not grown big. It's useful in the yard, being jockey size. Means I can ride anything from Shetland to cart'oss."

Nicky said she supposed it must be and glanced at her watch. Gone eleven. Hardly time now to sketch the badger. Zak's repair job, though, was well worth the sacrifice. Mum would never notice the join. She was about to ask Zak how he had acquired the skill when he choked on a splutter of laughter.

"What's so funny all of a sudden?" Nicky asked sharply.

Drawing a keen breath, Zak thrust his thin face closer and said eagerly, “D’you know, Nick? I got an ace idea!”

THREE

"It's like this," Zak began with an air of one-who-knows-all. "That Comet, well, he ain't no good for you. Right?"

Nicky gave a cautious nod.

Zak smiled craftily. "He's barely broke. A wild thing, out for trouble. Then there's you—green as grass!" He shook his head and tutted. "Two novices don't mix. My Cobber now, well, he's a saint. . ."

Nicky's throat went dry. She knew what was coming.

". . . So let's swap! Think about it. You said yourself how alike the two 'osses are. Both 12.2 hh, chestnut, medium-boned. Difference is my Cobber NEVER bucks, rears or bolts. What's more, he'll do all you ask at them rallies and gymkhanas. Regular schoolmaster, is my Cobber. He'd suit you perfect!"

The thought was dazzling. And then the warning bells rang, loud and clear in Nicky's mind. "But. . . but there's Mum," she said in a small, breathless voice. "Mum's no fool. She'll SEE it's a different pony."

Zak waved his hand airily. "Just don't you worry about

it, Nick. I can fix my Cobber so as your ma'll never know."

"But how?" Nicky cried, "Comet's all chestnut. Cobber's got a white blaze and sock."

"That ain't no problem!" assured Zak. "I'm tellin' you the honest truth. I can fix anything!"

Not entirely certain of his meaning, Nicky remained silent. And then it struck her. "You wouldn't DYE Cobber's coat?"

Zak shrugged. "Like I said, I can do anything with 'osses! If I fix that white it'll stay bright chestnut till my Cobber casts his hair."

"And what happens then?"

"We refix of course. I dunno, what a one you are for seeing problems where there ain't none!"

Nicky gnawed on her bottom lip. There were other factors to consider. "Comet's a young pony," she said. "How old is your Cobber?"

"He's in his prime." The reply was hedgy. "Got years in him yet!"

"And Cobber's mane and tail are bushier than Comet's."

"No problem! I can do him up trim as a thoroughbred. Honest!"

There was a long silence. Horribly tempted, Nicky stared down at the weedy cobblestones where the small flock of white hens had gathered to peck around their feet. Her common sense told her quite lucidly that swapping a thoroughbred pony for one of uncertain background was out of the question. There was the added problem of age. Even to her inexperienced eye. Cobber had a certain maturity over Comet. Mum would surely spot that? The whole venture was too risky. And yet…

Zak drew a deep breath and said fiercely, "Look, your Comet's a nutter. He needs taking back to basics. Schoolin' proper. Can you do that?"

Dismally Nicky shook her head.

"Then where's your problem?" cried Zak, leaping up in one fleet, graceful movement that sent the hens squawking off with an indignant flapping of wings. "Tell you what. Why don't I fetch Cobber an' you try him? Eh?"

Before Nicky could object Zak had flung her the mended rein and vanished into the stable. Nicky heaved a sigh. She supposed it could do no harm to try the pony.

Zak was back almost immediately, leading a sleepy Cobber by the forelock. With marked lack of enthusiasm, Nicky dragged herself to her feet. Her head swam a little. Although the pain had now gone, she was left with a peculiar lethargy and really the last thing she wanted was to be joggled about on a pony.

"We'll use your tack," Zak said, scooping up the bridle and deftly removing the bit. "But NOT this flamin' kimblewick. My Cobber wears a snaffle an' nothing else. If your ma objects, tell her it were your idea."

"Oh Zak, Mum'll have a. . ." Nicky began in wearied protest, but the boy was gone. Apprehensively she glanced at Cobber, who stood where Zak had left him, blinking his eyes against the sudden glare of the sun. He looked calm and quiet and at peace with himself. The very opposite to that wretch Comet.

Zak returned, dangling a shining jointed snaffle. Comet's new saddle was slung carelessly across his shoulders.

Nicky watched him fit the snaffle, and then Cobber was tacked up, with Zak giving a running commentary on what he was doing and why. The bridle was whipped on and fitted, so the bit lay snug and 'not pinchin' the poor 'oss's mouth'. The saddle was laid well up on Cobber's withers, then eased gently into place to 'make the hair lie good an' flat—you don't get the best out of an 'oss if it ain't comfy!'

"I'll say this for your ma," Zak muttered, his fingers approving the craftsman cut of the all-purpose saddle, "she's kitted that pony out with quality gear."

"You should have seen Fella's," Nicky replied tartly. "We weren't all that well off in those days. his saddle was ancient. And his bridle was made up from odd bits and pieces."

"Somethin' like mine, you mean?" Zak said with a laugh.

Nicky smiled, faintly. "Mum was determined to have Comet turned out as well as the others at Pony Club. She's bought royal blue day rugs and matching leg and tail bandages. His halter and lead rope are royal blue as well. And I've a dark blue jacket and toning silk for my hat—"

"Painted the stable door the same colour?" said Zak, grinning.

"Not yet!" Nicky found herself laughing, but felt moved to point out in defence of her mother, "Mum's really gone to a lot of trouble over the pony. She'll be heckish disappointed if I ruin everything with my useless riding."

"Well you won't, not on my Cobber, so don't fret about it!" Zak said surely, running a hand over the saddle. "You should soak this with oil to soften it. But not the seat mind, or you'll NEVER stay on!"

"I've used saddle soap," Nicky said in hurt tones. it seemed that nothing she did was right.

Zak buckled the girth, yanked down the stirrups and stepped back. "Get on then, Nick."

Cobber stood rock still, his dark eyes kind and wise and still a little sleepy, but Nicky hesitated. Now that the actual moment had come, the thought of mounting a pony—ANY pony—was frightening. Her heart began to thud uncomfortably and the palms of her hands went clammy. She felt the colour drain from her cheeks.

Zak grinned across at her reassuringly. "I'd put me gran on this little 'oss, he's that quiet," he encouraged. "Get on, I'll lead him a bit. A ride'll do your confidence a power a good."

This was true. With trembling fingers Nicky stroked Cobber's glossy neck. His coat was smoother than Comet's, most likely because he had always been correctly groomed. But then, Cobber was not inclined to bite or kick, which made a difference. The prospect of entering the loose-box without threat of being rammed into the middle of next week was suddenly sweet. Nicky grabbed the reins and scrambled clumsily into the saddle.

Zak clicked his tongue and the chestnut moved forward, down between the rows of pens. Nicky glanced over her shoulder to see the little sow badger shuffle back into her shed.

"She'll have a kip now till me gran gets in," Zak said. "Then they all wake up for their tea."

"I'd love to meet your gran," Nicky said quickly. "D'you think she'd let me stroke that badger?"

"Mebbe." Zak gave one his emphatic shrugs. "You never know with me gran. Depends whether or not she takes to you."

There was a busy clucking sound and the white hens came scuttling across their path in a tearing hurry. Cobber barely flinched, but Nicky made a startled grab for his mane.

"Relax," said Zak. "Honest Nick, my Cobber's bombproof."

Nicky loosed her grip slightly and Cobber plodded on. A hush was now descending on the yard as creatures settled down for their afternoon sleep. Rabbits, squirrel, hares and hedgehogs were now nowhere to be seen. The white goat dozed in a pool of sunlight. In the aviary sparrows, tits and finches perched in silent rows, feathers fluffed around their matchstick feet and beaks tucked in.

Only the grounded dogfox remained wakeful, his slanting golden eyes following them balefully as they went past.

Zak led Cobber through the orchard where the donkeys grazed and entered a wide, grassy field, patched with buttercups and enclosed by ragged hedges of hawthorn and holly. Beyond, the forest rose darkly. Nicky fixed her gaze firmly between Cobber's ears.

"Walk him round yourself now," Zak said, going to shut the gate. "Get the feel of him, like."

Nicky urged Cobber alongside the straggling hedge. His stride was smooth and comfortable, not at all like Comet's, which was jerky to the extreme. Nicky gave the pony's shoulder a cautious pat. He really was nice. The nervous flutterings inside her had all but disappeared and it was actually quite enjoyable, ambling over the grass, safe in the knowledge that one's mount would not resort to any nonsense.

It would be great to own Cobber, she thought longingly. But supposing she did exchange him for Comet and her mother found out? The consequences would be dire. Mum would never get over it—neither would Dad come to that, as Comet had cost him a lot of money. The dealer had said that Comet was exceptionally well-bred. He was by show stallion Starr Golden Rocket, out of Starr Shower of Gold. Who would have thought that two ponies with such terrific-sounding names could have produced such a demon?

The midday sun beat down. Nicky's scalp itched beneath her close-fitting hat and her long mouse-brown hair felt a dead weight on her shoulders.

They had meant to have Comet freeze-branded, but what with getting the house renovated and furnishings chosen, Mum had not come round to it. Maybe it was meant. Nicky's heart gave a familiar twist. She had always believed in things being meant. Mum laughingly called her fatalistic. Well, if meeting up with Zak and Cobber wasn't fate, she didn't know what was!

"ARE YOU DONKEY RIDIN' OR WHAT?" bellowed Zak cuttingly across the field. "GET HIM MOVIN'! THE POOR 'OSS IS FALLIN' ASLEEP!"

Nicky heaved a sigh and squared her shoulders. It was all right for Zak, to whom riding came as naturally as breathing. Lesser mortals like herself had to steel themselves to venture out of a plod.

Uncomfortably aware of Zak watching her every more, Nicky felt her right rein and used her legs, as they had been instructed at Pony Club. She was surprised and not a little pleased when Cobber sprang obediently forward and trotted a perfect circle. It was like being back on Fella only better, because Cobber was more willing. Gaining confidence, she trotted him on the other rein and then ambitiously attempted a rather squashed figure-eight.

"CANTER!" roared Zak impatiently. "LET HIM KNOW HE'S CARRYIN' A JOCKEY, NOT A BOWL O' JELLY!"

Nicky drew an indignant breath and, sitting tight, felt the reins and pushed hard with her legs. Cobber came in sweetly, his jaw flexed, his hocks under him. . . and they were cantering, light as air down the field. Nicky heard the grass swish rhythmically beneath the pony's hooves. Cobber made no attempt to buck, nor did he threaten to take hold and bomb off.

All too soon they reached the top of the field. Nicky steered the chestnut round and, following the trail they had made through the buttercups, cantered him gracefully back.

She dismounted. Her legs felt rubbery, her skin slick with sweat. She was still undecided, and it was all she could do to meet Zak's eyes.

"Well? What d'you make of him?"

Nicky stroked Cobber's neck, and when he responded by nuzzling her palm she felt an astonishing surge of affection flow through her. "Oh heck, he's so sweet," she said. "There's no comparison between him and Comet."

"No, there ain't!" agreed Zak wryly.

"Suppose you WERE to take Comet on," Nicky said, slowly and carefully, "and he turned out no good? What then?"

Zak shrugged. "That's my problem, ain't it? Anyway"—the grin was back—"there ain't been an 'oss yet what I couldn't master!"

Nicky could well believe it. "And there's this wretched jumping," she fretted. "I suppose Cobber does jump?"

"Like a stag!" was the prompt reply. "Want to try him?"

"No thanks!" Nicky paled. The fact that she had as much as mounted another pony after her experience with Comet was nothing short of a miracle. "I'm not experienced enough. You jump him, I'll watch."

In a far corner of the field a couple of rustic poles slung across rusted oil drums made a rough and ready fence. A few paces further on was another obstacle, which Zak had painted in lurid purple and pink stripes.

Zak vaulted lightly into the saddle, crossed the stirrups and whisked Cobber away over the grass. Seeing the jump, Cobber's ears pricked. He took off eagerly, soared, landed and went cantering gamely for the next, which he cleared with equal enthusiasm. Nicky could picture him in the ring, performing to the appreciative roaring of the crowd.

It was when she came to put herself on his back that the daydream fell apart.

Swinging Cobber in a tight circle, Zak popped him back the other way over both jumps and allowed him to canter on freely. A few yards or so from Nicky, the boy sprang neatly to his feet on to Cobber's rump, straightened, and, balancing with practised ease, sent the chestnut in a wide circle, exactly like a rosinback rider in a circus. Gathering himself, he then somersaulted off backwards over Cobber's tail and landed, nimbly upright on the grassy ground. The pony cantered another circle and Zak, meeting him, hurled himself back into the saddle.

Show off! thought Nicky. All the same, she was impressed.

Zak brought Cobber to a flamboyant halt beside her and jumped down. "Dead quiet, ain't he? And like I said, jumps anything. Fancy a go?"

Nicky eyed the rails dubiously. They looked huge, especially the painted ones.

"Oh flippin' heck, it's a rockin' horse you want!" Zak scoffed. "Get on him, I'll drop the poles."

It was not half as bad as she had feared. Adjusting himself to his rider, Cobber took the obstacles carefully, not jumping big and not tearing off when he reached the other side. Nicky was secretly delighted to find herself still in the saddle.

"Taken to him, ain't you?" Zak said.

Nicky was silent, her fingers playing in Cobber's mane. It felt rather coarse, not like Comet's which was quite fine. But then Mum wouldn't know that, because she had never had the trauma of grooming the beast.

"What d'you say then, Nick?"

Sensing her hesitation Zak bared a forearm and displayed a livid, purpling bruise. "That Comet's crackers, you know. Did I tell you he took a swipe at me just now, when I got the tack?"

"I'm not one bit surprised!" Nicky slithered to the ground. "I told you he's a pig. I can't think why you want him."

Zak was silent for a moment, then hammered his final advantage home. "When's your next rally?"

Nicky's heart sank. A violent quivering, like moths beating their wings, started up inside her. She really dreaded riding Comet in front of all those staring strangers on their well-schooled mounts. "Actually, it's tomorrow," she said shakily. "Oh heck! It'll be all chin AP, shewlders BECK!"

"Rugs ORN, rugs ORF?" Zak added.

Nicky caught his eye and Zak, giving a wild hoot, began to strut up and down, chest out, head high, in a brilliant imitation of the DC. His mood was infectious and, giggling, Nicky sprang into step beside him.

Both ended up shrieking with laughter. The sound carried and there was a stir of movement around the yard as the animals were wakened from their midday nap. On its heels came a disgruntled cheeping, grunting and squeaking, which gradually increased in volume. The dog inside the house began to bark and the donkeys, who had come to investigate the disturbance over the orchard gate, raised their whiskery chins and added a few rusty brays to the cacophony.

The din was unbelievable and Nicky clapped her hands over her ears. Zak evidently thought the whole thing hilarious, because his laughter now verged on the hysterical, his shoulders heaving, his breath coming in sobbing gasps and tears running in rivulets down his cheeks.

Totally overcome, Nicky staggered up to Cobber and giggled long and helplessly into his mane. She sobered at once when Zak's hand fell upon her shoulder.

"What about it, Nick? Is it a deal?" His grubby palm was thrust forward, and after a brief pause Nicky met it with her own in a resounding slap.

"It's a deal!" she hissed. "And Zak, as the next rally is tomorrow—"

Zak was quick. "Us'd best get to work!"

FOUR

"CHIN UP! SHOULDERS BACK! BOTTOM IN!" roared Mrs Parks-Harrison, standing foursquare in the middle of Chantley Manor's grassy paddock and tapping a silver-tipped riding whip against her jodhpured thigh. It was mid-morning and the District Commissioner was in full flow, her flinty eyes setting each rider in turn. Stiff and sore from the previous day, Nicky did her best to follow the instruction and managed to keep Cobber going in a steady circle, which was more than could be said for some of the other riders.

But then a picture of Zak giving his DC impression sprang to mind, and a nervous little splutter of mirth escaped her. All eyes turned her way and Mrs Parks-Harrison pounced.

"The new girl on the chestnut, um. . ."—she drew a list from her pocket and consulted it—"ah yes, Nicolette. You must CONCENTRATE! Sit UP dear. Lower your hands. Thumbs on top, that's MUCH better, now your pony is responding. Keep moving everybody. HANDS DOWN! KNEES IN! HEELS DOWN!"

The circling continued and Nicky swallowed a yawn. She had lain awake half the night, wrestling with her conscience. What if her mother found out about Comet? Should she have swapped him? She knew the answer of course, but that had only proved to make matters worse. When she had finally slept it was to dream absurdly of floundering in a deep bowl of jelly, with Zak mocking her from the saddle of a stamping fiery-eyed horse.

"Remember, don't tie Cobber up," had been Zak's parting shot as she had ridden the freshly 'fixed' chestnut from the yard.

Reaching home a good two hours late, Mum had greeter her anxiously and had even, to Nicky's dismay, helped turn the pony out, a thing she had never done before. Fortunately Cobber had strolled to a distant corner, sniffed the ground and promptly rolled as if he had lived at The Briars all his life. Mum had even remarked upon how well he had settled in.

Luck was on her side this morning, too. Mum had been in such a spin, packing lunch and fussing over appearances—those boots are NOT shiny enough, give them another polish. Why aren't you wearing a clean shirt? Nicolette, that is NOT the way to fix your tie. Come here, let me!—that she had been too hassled to bother with the pony. Nicky had flicked a brush over him and hawked him unceremoniously into the new trailer.

It was significant that her headache had not returned. For this Nicky was grateful and she made up her mind to thank Zak's grandmother at the earliest opportunity. She also wanted to satisfy her curiosity about the wildlife at

Keeper's Lodge. And she was desperate to draw that badger.

"PREPARE TO TROT! TRRRROT!" shouted the DC. The ponies lurched forward with a great deal of huffing and head-tossing and flitching of tails.

Because she was new, Nicky had been placed into the D-Group, which was the most novice. "But not for long," Mrs Parks-Harrison had encouraged. "Work hard and pass your D-Test, then you will progress to more interesting areas, like jumping and cross country."

Frankly Nicky doubted it, but with a fixed smile and hammering heart had urged Cobber into the group of struggling novices. She and Cobber were squashed between sturdy, frank-faced Roger Davies on Dutchman, his cobby piebald, and slim, dark-haired Lisa Scott on Moonspinner, her glossy black show pony. Nicky rather liked Roger, who had a friendly smile and warm brown eyes.

Roger's mother, Nicky discovered, was the Honorary Secretary for the club. Bespectacled and efficient, Mrs Davies spent her time haring from one group to the next with frightfully important messages.

Opposite were Daniel and Tom Flynn, twin boys with reddish hair and round, cheerful faces. They were mounted on Punch and Snippet, stocky Exmoors with short legs, mealy noses and profuse manes and tails. The ponies were incredibly naughty and kept bucking and unshipping their riders, to the veiled amusement of the group and the DC's exasperation.

There were several extremely small children on fat unwieldy Shetlands. One Shetland, Nicky noticed with surprise, was ridden by a girl of about her own age. This pony, a gleaming mahogany black, was nifty and remarkably well schooled. The girl, shabbily dressed in patched jods and a jacket that had seen better days, contrasted strongly with the other smartly attired riders. Sharp grey eyes glinted from beneath the peak of an old-fashioned crash hat, which might once have been her mother's, and her lace-up shoes were polished to a fine shine. She managed her pony expertly and with obvious enjoyment.

Beyond the paddocks rose Chantley Manor. Timbered and ancient, with mullioned windows and vast, crazily-twisting chimneys, it looked snug and welcoming. The prancing unicorn coat-of-arms was carved into stone over each studded oak door. Surrounding the house, rambling gardens gave off on to trim orchards and white railed paddocks.

Immaculate stables, approached beneath a clock-arch, flanked a paved yard. Only half the loose-boxes were in use, the rest being shuttered and closed, a sad reminder of more affluent times.

A winding, tree-lined drive led to the house. Nicky had not missed the gleam of appreciation in her mother's eye when they had first approached.

Fierce concentration radiated from the line of parked cars and trailers, from which the parents watched with critical interest. Turning her head to pick out her mother brought Nicky another reprimand from the DC. "Nicolette! You are daydreaming again and your pony is falling asleep. Sit up dear. Use your legs."

Nicky obeyed. Cobber responded promptly, surging forward nicely on the bit, his jaw flexing, hocks under him.

"HEAPS better! Good gel. What a super pony you have." Mrs Parks-Harrison's praise was gushing. But there was no respite, and the next command was called briskly. "Everyone prepare to canter. Don't forget to keep a pony's length between you and the one in front. CANTER!"

Cobber altered his stride and when Nicky found herself going crash-lurch-slip in Comet's new saddle, she realized that she had forgotten about not oiling the seat. Zak was right again.

"SIT TIGHT! HANDS DOWN!" roared the DC, going onto admonish the Flynn twins when their Exmoors once more exploded into mischievous little bucks. The two boys were scarlet and one of them had the audacity to pull a face behind the DC's back. How she saw was impossible to tell, but the ticking off she gave him was dire.

She's like a dragon, groaned Nicky silently. A horny one with eyes in the back of her head, breathing fire on the innocents.

There was a brief stop for a latecomer, a girl on a Welsh-type dappled grey, who slipped into the circle with a nervous apology.

"Annis Reed." The DC ticked off the girl's name on her list. Annis was pretty, with curly golden hair, wide green eyes and a powdering of freckles over her nose. Nicky smiled at her and Annis grinned back.

"ANNIS, PLEASE CONCENTRATE!" bawled the DC at once. Startled, Annis lost a stirrup and her pony stopped dead. The Shetland following promptly shot sideways and made off, hell-bent for home with its rider bouncing precariously in the overlarge saddle. Back in the ring chaos reigned, with Shetlands taking root and the other ponies milling, hopelessly out of control, their red-faced riders kicking and tugging in futile desperation.

"ORDER! ORDER!" bellowed the DC, bearing down on them in such fury that Nicky fully expected a jet of green flame to spurt from her mouth. "Rein in, everyone. Tom Flynn, will you get that pony under control? And you, Daniel! WHOA THERE!"

Nicky, who had succeeded in halting Cobber away from the turmoil, watched as the DC efficiently sorted everyone out.The escaped Shetland, its rider miraculously still aboard, was firmly escorted back by a breathless mother, and the torture began again. "Chin up. Shoulders back. Bottom in. . ."

Curled by the paddock rails was Bess, the Parks-Harrisons' elderly yellow Labrador. Bess, who had attended countless rallies, slept through the activity with blissful unconcern.

In the adjoining paddocks, three other groups were being worked expertly and with MUCH concentration. Mrs Parks-Harrison's daughter, Pru, who was newly qualified in equine studies, instructed dressage. The family's mature and much-respected groom, Dobson—fondly known to everyone as Dobs—was teaching working hunter tactics in a calm, measured voice. Dobs was slight and stooped, with a kindly, weatherbeaten face. His legs were very bowed in their old-fashioned, baggy breeches, and his arms, jutting from the rolled-up sleeves of his checked shirt, were brown and sinewy.

Road safety was taken by a plumpish, red-haired woman in skin-tight white trousers and tee-shirt, whom

Nicky later found out was Mrs Patsy Flynn, qualified instructor and mother of the cheerful twins. Nicky decided that Mrs Flynn looked good fun and so, for that matter, did Pru and Dobs. It was just the DC.

A halt for lunch was called at last. Riders were made to line up, dismount and stand at their pony's head, while the DC strode through the ranks giving yet more advice. Tom Flynn was given detailed counsel upon how to teach his pony to stop. They were then told to lead off.

Nicky led Cobber across the grass, to where her mother waited with the new hatchback and trailer.

"Didn't Comet go WELL?" Mum enthused, leaping out of the car, blue headcollar in hand. She was elegant in a designer leisure suit, with her face carefully made up and her wavy hair tamed to a smooth bob.

Nicky sighed. Actually her mother looked fine, and she was only following the trend of all the other parents, but somehow Nicky felt sad. The jeans-and-shirt-clad Mum of the old days would have been quick to lend a hand with the younger riders, instead of languishing in the car.

"Weren't you bored, just watching?" Nicky asked.

Mum shook her head. "I enjoyed it. All this planning and sorting out at home is tiring. It's good to have a day off."

Nicky was standing, flexing her aching muscles and debating upon whether or not her legs would carry her the last few steps to the car, when she realized that her mother had taken Cobber, whipped the halter over his bridle and was about to tether him to the side of the trailer.

"DON'T!" Forgetting her aches and pains Nicky

launched herself forward and snatched the rein from her mother's astonished grip.

"Whatever's wrong?" asked Mum crossly.

"C. . . Comet won't tie up," In her panic Nicky almost stammered the wrong name. "He pulls back and. . . he might break his halter."

"But I've seen Comet tied, often," her mother protested. "What notions you get!"

Treacherous colour flooded Nicky's cheeks. "Yes well, he used to tie up but. . . but the other day something spooked him and he's been stupid ever since," she fibbed.

"Oh," said her mother lamely. "I daresay he'll get over it." She watched Nicky march the pony up the ramp into the safety of the trailer and then, with a little dismissive shrug, turned her attention to the lunch. This, as she was attempting to convert her family to healthy eating, was salad and granary rolls followed by fruit.

Nibbling the gritty bread, Nicky cast an envious eye on the Flynns, parked adjacent to them. Mother and boys were tucking ravenously into doorstep sandwiches, sausage rolls, crisps and thickly buttered scones.

Nicky sighed. Although she quite liked her mother's health meals, today she would have preferred what her father bluntly called 'proper food.'

"Muesli slice?" Mum offered brightly. Nicky shook her head in glum refusal.

"DO cheer up, Nicolette," Mum coaxed with a reproachful sigh. "You're supposed to be ENJOYING yourself!"

Nicky bit her lip. She wished her mother would stop using her full name. She always used to call her Nicky like everyone else did. And as to being miserable, well, privately Nicky considered that she and Cobber had got through the morning rather well, with only a couple of mild reprimands from the DC. All due to Cobber, of course. He had been a wonder so far, responding without protest to her clumsy aids and not putting a hoof wrong, just as Zak had promised.

"I must admit you do look after Comet well," Mum was saying. "His condition HAS improved. His coat seems glossier."

Nicky turned away as guilty colour once more flushed her cheeks. She must remember to call the pony Comet, not Cobber, she told herself. Twice she had almost slipped up and Mum had snapped at her for speaking indistinctly!

Comet. Comet. Comet. . . Nicky reasoned that if she repeated the name often enough in her head, that would do the trick. But somehow it did not, because gentle Cobber was nothing like that other wretch.

An elbow dig brought her attention. "The DC's coming. For pity's sake, Nicolette, don't look so gloomy." Mum curved her own lips into a welcoming smile and wound down the window.

"Hello there!" said Mrs Parks-Harrison, stooping so that her squarish, outdoor face was level with theirs. "Mrs McGuire?"

"Karen," Nicky's mother reminded her.

"Ah yes, Karen. Everything fine?"

It was more a statement than a question. "Of course," Mum agreed with a slightly forced laugh. "We're enjoying ourselves tremendously, aren't we Nicolette?"

Somehow, Nicky contrived to convey her enthusiasm for the rally and the DC smiled. "I just love your pony," she said. "He's a true schoolmaster, exactly what you need to begin with. How clever of you to come across him. Reminds me rather of the Lady Helen Mosscrop's Bellmaster Supreme. Lovely pony, that. Worth his weight in gold. Do you know Helen?"

"Er, unfortunately no," said Mum, faintly.

"Delightful gel," recalled the DC. "Seventy if she's a day, you know, and still does her own stables..."

Nicky switched off. Her gaze strayed to the Manor and its vivid gardens. If only she had brought her sketch-book. The house would be a perfect subject. She rather like drawing buildings; it was so satisfying, getting the perspective correct and the shadows falling the correct way. . .

"Your group is having Pru next." Nicky surfaced blankly to find the DC addressing her. "Pru does mounted games. Super fun, you and Comet will enjoy it immensely!"

FIVE

She was right.

Blonde and bubbly, Pru had a fantastic sense of humour and a terrific way with ponies—and their riders.

"Now listen, you lot," she said, standing with her hands planted firmly on her slim, black-jodhpured hips. "It's time Chantley did something else apart from hunting and showing. I want to get up a Prince Philip Team. It will be great fun, and at the same time it will teach you horsemanship. Anyone interested?"

The roar of response was tremendous. Ponies' ears shot forward. The black show pony began to paw the ground and the little Exmoors wheeled in excited circles. Nicky was thrown into panic. Zak had not mentioned mounted games. Supposing Cobber was not experienced in these?

"Does that mean no more circling?" piped up Tom Flynn, whom Nicky had overheard protesting loudly to his mother that his pony only bucked from sheer boredom.

"Not exactly," Pru returned. "We'll be doing the team games for training. It will help if you work your ponies at home—vaulting on, starting and stopping, neck-reining and so on. Oh, and get them used to noises—balloons bursting, hooters, that sort of thing."

"I'll have to teach Snippet to stop!" Tom wailed in despair.

Pru laughed. "You're quite right, stoppability is vastly important. Ponies must also be supple, fit and well-balanced to cope with the twists and turns. Speed is a factor, too. Ponies AND riders must be athletic—"

"A hundred press-ups morning and night!" Tom hissed in Snippet's ear. There was a ripple of laughter. Everyone was cheering up. Even Nicky felt a spark of interest.

"Temperament must be good," Pru continued. "Ponies should be unflappable and willing. I take it all your mounts are over four years of age?"

"Punch is six," Daniel put in. His twin informed that Snippet was a year older. Moonspinner was five, Lisa said faintly. The others, busily counting on their fingers, each eventually came up with some age. Only Nicky remained silent.

Pru cast a critical eye over their tack. "Martingales and nosebands are allowed in the games. No whips or spurs, however. Oh, and ponies MUST be ridden in snaffles, so don't be tempted to try other bits if your mount isn't responding. It remains to be seen if your ponies are up to it."

Some of the sparkle left her grey eyes and she sighed. "I had a brilliant gymkhana pony once. A skewbald called Dandy. Nothing much to look at, stocky, scruffy mane and tail, you know the sort? Wouldn't pass muster in a showing class, but could he do mounted games. . .?" She paused significantly.

"Where is he now?" Daniel wanted to know.

"I wish I could tell you!" Pru said. "He disappeared one night from the paddock. We tried all ways to trace him. Adverts, police, trailing the auctions. Mother even offered a reward, but it was no good, he'd just vanished. I didn't dare think what might have happened to him."

An uncomfortable stillness fell over the group. Pru gave a little shrug. "It happened years ago. NOW," she continued in a lighter vein, "you all know Chantley Horse Show and Gymkhana?"

"YES!" came the cry in unison.

"Then let's make that our goal. At Chantley Show each of you must enter EVERY mounted game and qualify not only for the finals, but gain either a first or second in these. Then I'll know whether you are worth training or not. If you should all get chucked out then I'll forget it."

The twins groaned. Everyone else assumed determined stares.

"Some of you may be aware of this, but for the benefits of the others I'll explain. We need six riders for a Prince Philip team—the minimum's five, but I prefer six. I shall also need some reserves, but I can pull these from the other groups if need be. Likewise ponies. IF we make up a team, then you'll have to work jolly hard ALL the time, because we have to qualify in the Area competition in the spring. Ours is held at Ludlow. There will be inter-team competitions, too—good for experience, these. Then we go for the Zone, and finally, WEMB-

LEY!"

Spurred by her enthusiasm everyone cheered, even the little ones who had no idea of what Pru was talking about. Pru fixed the small, solemn-faced riders with a direct gaze and said kindly, "Obviously some of you are rather young, but don't worry, Mrs Flynn has offered to take charge of leading-rein gymkhana, so that I can concentrate on the oldies. Guess we'll deal with you first. Now, little ones on small fattie ponies..."

Diligently Pru began to sort them out. Mrs Flynn bounded up and, with the assistance of several mothers roped in by Pru, swept ponies and riders away. Nicky glanced to see if her mother was offering help but no, Mum still sat in the car. She was reading a magazine now, as she was not interested in gymkhana games.

To distinguish the two sections, Pru called them the Smalls on Shetlands and the Rest.

The gymkhana equipment was ancient and battered, the sacks frayed, the faded wooden cones and bending posts pitted with worm-holes. Whilst Pru helped Dobs to sort it out, Nicky grabbed a word with Annis Reed.

"Is this your first season, too?"

Annis nodded. "My second rally, though. My Dad's a blacksmith. He's offered to be on call at rallies and gymkhanas, we get our subs reduced that way. Mum thinks Pony Club's a bit expensive. It isn't that she begrudges the money, she just believes there are better ways of spending it."

Nicky searched for some answer to this, failed utterly and came up with, "Useful, having a farrier for a dad."

"Blacksmith!" Annis corrected with a smile. "Dad does welding as well as shoeing horses. Yes, it is useful in lots of ways. Grooms are ace gossips so we get all the news. It's great!"

Her round eyes glinted. But then the DC's voice carried, loud and threatening form the jumping manege, and the two girls exchanged a meaningful glance.

"Bit of a tyrant, isn't she?" said Nicky.

Annis laughed. "She's a good teacher though. She's turned out some ace riders."

Nicky went on to admire Annis's pony. Actually, as the grey was beautifully dappled and extremely kind-looking she found herself talking with truth, which was gratifying as only yesterday she had never wanted to look at another horse again. Tiffin enjoyed mounted games, Annis said. Her dad had fixed up bending poles in the corner of their field and they practised a lot. How about Nicky's chestnut?

"Co. . . Comet?" Nicky coloured. Would she ever get that name right? "Oh, I haven't a clue what he can do and as I'm a complete novice, I suppose anything can happen."

"You must come and have a go at our place," Annis offered promptly. "It'll be more fun with two of us. That is, providing you don't mind the Tinies."

Nicky stared blankly, and Annis gestured towards the row of parked vehicles where, in the shade of a spreading copper beech, there stood an oldish trailer and basic family car. Annis' Mother evidently did not waste money on plush runabouts either, was Nicky's first thought. Sprawled on the grass was a young-looking woman with healthy red cheeks and masses of untidy fair hair. She was chatting to three chubby toddlers, who were dressed identically in shorts and tee-shirts.

"My sisters," Annis informed. "They're triplets. Angie, Annabel and Andrea, born in that order. They're three now, and terrible!" A smile took the sting out of this last statement.

Each child was fresh-faced and dimpled, with huge green eyes and blonde corkscrew curls.

"Our Mum baby-minds too, for mothers who go out to work," Annis said. "You can tell which is our cottage because it's the noisiest. It's at the end of the village, black'n'white and squashed looking on account of the old beams. . . Something wrong?"

Nicky had stiffened. The word cottage had thrown her back to the North. She could almost feel the cool waft of the fell breeze fanning her hot cheek, and was subsequently gripped by an overwhelming sense of homesickness. But Annis was regarding her curiously, so she forced a shrug. "Wrong? No, nothing wrong at all!"

Pru shouted then. "Line up, you idle bunch, let's have a look at you!"

Everyone surged forward. Roger Davies on piebald Dutchman; Lisa Scott on her black show pony, Moon-spinner; Daniel and Tom Flynn with Punch and Snippet; Annis on Tiffin and Nicky on Cobber. Pru frowned towards the wiry girl in scruffy clothes. Her Shetland's name, it turned out, was Dinah Mite.

"Mo Stephens, isn't it?" Pru enquired after glancing at her list.

The girl said yes. she spoke with a lisp, due to a brace on her front teeth. Dinah Mite's small ears were pricked alertly, her eyes watchful beneath the shaggy fall of mane. Pru, after consulting her list again, said dubiously, "Mother's noted here your pony's a crack hand at mounted games. Is this true?"

"You bet!" Mo grinned, showing a mouthful of steel plate.

Darting the Shetland a doubtful glance, Pru waved them all towards the prepared ring and the fun began, fast and furious, with Musical Sacks.

Music was provided by Pru's powerful but temperamental machine which tended to jam, causing more pauses than was necessary. The grounds echoed to the lively beat of massed brass bands—and spasmodically to Pru's cursing as she fiddled in exasperation with the controls.

There was great hilarity from the far corner where Smalls on Shetlands were being drilled in leading-rein gymkhana. Mrs Flynn looked fearfully hot, racing beside the fast-trotting ponies.

"I shall lose POUNDS!" she shrieked for all to hear. "By the end of summer I'll be positively SYLPH-LIKE!"

"Thin Flynn!" sniggered Daniel.

"Instead of Fat Pat!" finished Tom.

"Less yapping and more work!" Pru ordered briskly. "If you boys put your energies into controlling those Exmoors instead of ridiculing your long-suffering mother, they'd be better behaved!"

No one minded the odd spill from an excited pony—except Lisa, whose thoroughbred jinked and fretted and grew steadily worse as the afternoon progressed.

"I'm most awfully sorry," Lisa wailed, picking herself up from the ground and examining the grass stains on her white jods. "But I can't seem to manage him."

Pru, having caught a sweating, eye-rolling Moonspinner, offered a leg-up. She asked, "What are you feeding him? He seems corned-up to me."

"I'm not sure. Mummy does him," Lisa confessed, going slightly pink.

Pru's brows drew together in a frown. "That's not on," she said. "You are old enough, and should be concerned enough, to look after your pony yourself."

"I'm awfully sorry," Lisa said again, miserably.

Pru snorted. "no oats in future! Now let's get on. MUSIC!"

The band blared. Dinah Mite proved an absolute riot, bouncing stoically round on her short hairy legs with her mane and tail flying in all directions. Cobber's ears, Nicky discovered, flicked the second the music stopped, when he tore to the centre and claimed a sack by cleverly placing his hoof on the nearest and standing firm, his flanks heaving, his breath coming in mighty huffs. Time and again Nicky won.

"You've a MADE gymkhana pony there!" Pru screamed, mopping her damp face with the back of her hand. "Gosh, I'm parched. Take a break, everyone. I'm going to find us a swig of something."

Riders slithered thankfully down. Ponies were patted. Nicky pulled Cobber's reins over his head and told him firmly to stand. When the chestnut obeyed there were gasps of surprise. Pru stopped in her tracks. "Did you teach him that?"

Nicky was saved from answering by Tiffin, who, staring doe-eyed at Dinah Mite, uttered a loud, grumpy huffle.

"What now?" enquired Pru with wearied patience.

"It's Tiffin," Annis said. "He sounds all cross but he isn't, he's a very placid character."

"Oh?" Pru was mystified. "Then what's he moaning about?"

Annis went crimson. "I think he's fallen in love with Dinah Mite!"

There was a spontaneous burst of laughter. "I can see I've got my work cut out with you lot!" Pru muttered, half-laughing, half-exasperated. She stalked off.

Daniel Flynn watched her retreating figure with reserve. "She's a bit of a slave driver," he complained. "Our ponies aren't up to this sort of thing. Neither am I."

"I'll NEVER be able to stop Snippet," Tom declared. "I have to yank him in a circle to pull him up, and that's no good for mounted games."

Roger eyed his piebald concernedly. "I think at 13.2hh Dutchman's big." He glanced at Nicky. "What height's your chestnut?"

"'Bout 12.2," she guessed.

"Tiffin's 12.1hh with his shoes," said Annis smugly. "Just right for mounted games."

The twins' ponies were the same. So was Lisa's Moonspinner. Mo listened to all this mutely. A Shetland, however good, was unlikely to make a PP team.

"I wonder what happens if your pony goes lame?" Tom wondered.

"I think established teams have several ponies apiece," said Mo. She shrugged hopelessly. "Fat chance of me getting even one more, unless Dad comes up with the pools."

There was an awkward silence. Annis looked uncomfortable. Her mum did not relish spending money on ponies. Tiffin had come to them by sheer chance, her dad being paid in kind by a client who had gone bankrupt.

Lisa heaved a fretful sigh. "Actually, Mummy mightn't be keen on Moonspinner doing games in case it ruins his legs."

"Then why bother?" asked Daniel bluntly.

Lisa shrank at his tone. "I wanted to try it," she protested. "I'd like to sell Moonspinner and buy something ordinary, like Tiffin." She shot the pony a covetous glance, but Annis, who objected to Tiffin being dubbed ordinary, gave a sniff.

Pru came back then with Dobs in tow, bearing a small barrel of home-brewed ginger beer and a pack of disposable beakers. Pru carried a jug of cider for Mrs Flynn who, she joked as she handed it to her, looked as though she needed something more sustaining.

"I'll get drunk!" Mrs Flynn chortled. "I'll pass the rest of the afternoon in a stupor!"

The ginger beer was sharp and cool and riders gulped it down thirstily. Tom offered Snippet his and cracked up laughing when the bubbles tickled the pony's nostrils, making him snort and rub his nose on Tom's sleeve. The liquid splashed everywhere.

"Now look what you've done!" Tom muttered, mopping at his tweed jacket, his white shirt, his Pony Club tie.

"Serves you right!" Pru retorted. "You're not getting any more either. Drink up, everyone! Let's get on!"

Next came bending. Nicky found Annis strong competition as Tiffin had daily experience of this at home. Even so, Cobber knew the game, and wove between the line of poles confidently. It was Nicky who hampered him, yawing his mouth and bouncing inexpertly in the saddle.

"Sit still, leave him alone and he'll do everything for you," Pru counselled sharply.

For the next game Pru had chosen Walk, Trot and Gallop which, she explained, was marvellous for learning control. Tom and Daniel, complained that it was boring. Shooting a daggered look, Pru ordered them into line.

Moonspinner, finding himself next to Dinah Mite, took a sudden dislike to her and started to back. Pru's patience was by now stretched to a fine thread, and she brusquely sent Lisa to the other end of the row. This put Tiffin next to Dinah Mite and grumpy huffles, so loud and so passionate, rang the length of the paddock. Faces under the peaked silks split into grins.

"I give up!" said Pru in amused exasperation. "For goodness' sake, Annis, take him to the end of the row."

"Which end?"

"EITHER!" Pru gasped.

"I guess this'd make an ace game," cut in Tom.

'You bet," said his twin. "'Cept eventually we'd all move down and the row'd disappear into the lake!"

Everyone laughed. Pru battled to keep a straight face. "For those not familiar with this game," she began through gritted teeth. "Remember to keep at a walking pace to the far line. If you break into a trot, you must circle your pony. The same rules apply for trotting. Galloping, you just go flat out. All clear?"

They prepared themselves for the starting whistle. As Pru had supposed, the game really sorted out the riders' control—or lack of it. The Flynns, whose ponies flatly refused to walk, had to pivot so many circles they were soon disqualified. Moonspinner kept backing into the other ponies and reduced Lisa to floods of tears. To Roger's delight, Dutchman did splendidly. Cobber and Tiffin performed well, too, being forced to circle only due to the incompetency of their riders. Dinah Mite executed a perfect walk and trot, but failed on the gallop as her short legs were no match for the bigger ponies.

"Guess we've a lot of work ahead," warned Pru. "Let's have a crack at an Obstacle Race. Nicky, Annis and Roger, a hand with gear, please. We'll need sacks, cones, skipping ropes. . ."

Her energy was boundless. It grew hotter. The afternoon flashed by and it was turned four when Pru finally called a halt.

"Thank goodness! I'm absolutely DEAD!" groaned Mrs Flynn, who promptly collapsed into a heap on the ground. There was no reply from her helpers who, by their already prostrate forms, felt much the same.

"You unfit creatures!" said Pru. "Wait till we're in training for real, then you'll know what work is all about!"

Pru turned to her group and gave them a brief pep talk, in which she assured them that they were not without hope. This was heartening, and she left them cheerfully gathering together the gymkhana gear.

"You will come?" Annis reminded Nicky as they watched Dobs cart it away. "Come on Sunday, about nine. We can go for a hack."

"I'll be there," Nicky promised eagerly.

"Who's that girl!" Mum asked, sliding the key into the

ignition.

Nicky told her. "Annis has invited me over to ride."

Mum cast the Reed's battered but functional outfit a tight look, but smiled at the sight of the three rounded little backsides, jostling to get into the car. She turned to Nicky with a smile. "I'm glad you've made a friend," she said. "I know you didn't really want to leave Appleby."

Nicky sat in mutinous silence.

"You WILL settle here, you know. It's always hard at first."

"It's just. . ." Nicky began awkwardly. "It's just that Chantley's so closed in after the fells. All these trees—"

"But the forest is beautiful," her mother said. "So is the village. All those quaint black and white cottages straddling the green. And the little allsorts shop and the lovely old church. It's all so timeless, with precious little traffic to bother the ponies. And think what a prize you've got in Comet. Why, when I was young I'd have given anything for a pony as good as he is!"

Driving home, Mum admitted that she had found the gymkhana games quite entertaining to watch after all. "Comet did well, didn't he? He's calmed down a lot." She laughed then, and exclaimed brightly to Nicky's horror, "In fact he's changed so much he might almost be a different pony!"

SIX

The next morning was dull and chilly. Nicky shivered as she placed the saddle on to Cobber's withers and slid it into place, the way Zak had done. Out of choice she would have waited until the day warmed up, but her mother had shooed her out. A pony should be exercised to a morning routine, Mum insisted. Not at its rider's leisure.

Nicky supposed she was right. At least there were less flies. Eavesdropping on the chat yesterday, it appeared that most people fell out of bed and on to their pony. Roger had confessed to keeping Dutchman stabled in the garage overnight, to save the bother of fetching the piebald up from the field.

It was not until Cobber was tacked up that Nicky realized that she had not groomed him from yesterday, so she hurriedly swept a brush over his dusty quarters. Leading him from the loose-box, she mounted stiffly and urged him on to the lane.

It was such a relief to be hacking along without fear of being thrown or bombed off with. Nicky felt a definite lift of spirits as she glanced about, her artist's eye assessing the subtle play of light and shade on the lushness of pastureland, the acres of ripening corn and the distant purpling hills.

Finches twittered in the hedgerow and overhead a flock of martins wheeled in little chittering flights, as if they were playing chase on the air currents. Cobber picked his patient way, head down and unhurried towards the forest. Nicky planned to call at Keeper's Lodge and tell Zak about the rally. More importantly, she hoped that his grandmother would be there.

Absently she wondered what Zak's gran would be like. Horsy and tweed-clad maybe, with a loud voice like the DC. Or gypsyish like Zak. Secretive. The sort of character you never quite got to know, however hard you tried.

Zak had inferred that she was not always the most sociable of persons. Well, Nicky was prepared to risk that. It would be worth it for the chance of stroking the little badger. It dawned on Nicky then that she had not picked up her sketchbook and pens. She had left them ready on the kitchen table, but Mum had tidied them away.

"Drat!" she muttered. 'Drat! Drat! Drat!"

Five minutes and she was trotting beneath the spreading oaks and sycamores of the Wyre Forest. Sensing his old home, Cobber quickened his pace. "Steady boy," Nicky said, nervously, as Comet's bolting tendencies were fresh in her mind. But a slight check on the rein was all it took to bring Cobber to a walk. Nicky gave his neck a rewarding pat.

Gaining Keeper's Lodge, Nicky had just dismounted to wrestle with the gate when a lean grey wolfhound came bounding across the yard, barking ferociously. It stopped a yard or so away, its hackless rising, lips curling in a vicious snarl. There was a gleam of sharp, white fangs. Cobber was unconcerned, but Nicky froze. The hound padded closer, huge and formidable, its yellow eyes glinting beneath the wispy fringe of hair. A menacing growl rumbled, deep in its throat. Nicky held her breath.

"HOUDINI! GET INSIDE!" shrieked a sudden voice. The dog dropped to the ground, turned its shaggy head reproachfully and slunk away, tail between its legs. Nicky watched until it had sidled indoors and then let out her breath in one rush of relief.

There came the clatter of milk pails. Heart still thumping painfully, Nicky glanced up to see a small, trim figure emerging from the goatshed.

It was her hair that struck Nicky first—a bright and unlikely shade of chestnut, and suspiciously reminiscent of the dye that Zak had used on Cobber's white blaze and sock. Floral culottes and pink tee-shirt with 'I'm a Greenie' splashed across the front furthered the youthful image. On her feet were a pair of black wellingtons, which looked several sizes too large.

Nicky fumbled with the knotted string that held the gate. The wellies were now squelching and squeaking over the dewy cobblestones, scattering hens left, right and centre. The milk pail was dumped inside the back door and the wellies made their squelching, squeaking progress closer. By now Nicky had managed the gate and was leading Cobber in.

The woman came to a stop. Vivid eyes, same blue as Zak's but lacking their guile, glittered in her lively, sun-browned face. "Ponies, is it?" she said sharply, glancing at Cobber without a hint of recognition and then fixing Nicky with a hard stare. "I reckon you'll be wanting Zak?"

"Well, sort of," Nicky replied, gulping. "I'm Nicky McGuire."

"And I'm Marcia Shone!" the woman revealed briskly. "Call us Marcia, everyone else does. Afraid Zak's out, but if you want to wait. . .?"

"Please," Nicky accepted. "But. . . but actually Zak said to come over and see you. I was here the other day and I noticed your animals. I just can't seem to stop thinking about them!" She hurried the words out breathlessly. Despite the fierce dog and Marcia's unfriendly approach, she was determined to discover more about the badger. "I hoped. . . er, Marcia. . . I wondered if you would please show me round?"

There was the very briefest of pauses, in which Nicky felt herself under close scrutiny. Lifting her chin, she held the woman's gaze levelly. She saw approval flicker in the blue eyes and was then favoured with a beaming smile.

"Just you come indoors, Nicky," said Marcia, warmly. "We'll have a cuppa, you and me. An' a chat!"

She reached out a firm hand and Nicky was powerless to prevent herself from being marched across the yard, Cobber in tow. Stabling him took a while, as the first shed housed a lame goose which hissed threateningly. The second held a ragged-looking donkey with a cute foal at foot, which they paused to admire.

"Third time lucky," Marcia cried, flinging wide the door of the next shed. And it was. Cobber was untacked and, leaving him hay, Marcia hustled Nicky over the cobblestones to the house.

"You have to take us as you find us," Marcia warned. "We don't stand on ceremony at Keeper's Lodge!"

One step inside and Nicky knew what she meant. The scuffed oak door gave off directly on to a squarish, dark-beamed living kitchen, its flagged floor dotted with hand-woven rugs, the narrow windows brightly curtained in chintz. The furniture was homely, a scrubbed table and set of Windsor chairs taking much of the space. But it was the clutter; the books and sewing and dusty piles of magazines littering every surface that grabbed Nicky's interest.

Breathtaking heat rolled across the room from an ancient black range, where a great fire roared. On one of the two easy chairs was curled a hugely-pregnant tabby cat. Houdini, sprawled on the hearthrug, raised his grizzled head and gave his rat-tail a cautious thump. Nicky edged past him warily.

"Sit down, Nicky," said Marcia, stomping across to the stove regardless of her muddied wellies and reaching for the kettle and teapot. "That is, if you can find an empty chair!"

Dumping a pile of newspapers on to the table, Nicky sat and stole another delighted glance around her. A vast oak dresser was laden with unusual and rather beautiful hand-cast pottery, all bearing Green messages. The top shelf displayed an intriguing array of jars and bottles, each carefully labelled. Nicky was quick to pick out the headache remedy. In a corner beside a pile of snowy fleece stood a spinning wheel, and steaming pungently over the fireplace were a couple of hanks of newly-washed wool.

No telephone, no radio, no television set. A room for doing things, Nicky decided.

Decking one wall was a bewildering assortment of horse gear; whips, bits, martingales, nosebands. . . and others Nicky could not put a name to. There was a glorious smell of leather, mingling with something baking in the side-oven. Nicky's mouth watered.

"Apple pie," Marcia said, going to open the oven door. She peeped in. "Done to a turn. We'll have a slice."

As she cut into the flaky crust there was a mighty scuffle from the hearth and Houdini came to rest his chin on Nicky's lap. His eyes shone with a warm amber light, and were so wise and wistful that she quite forgot her fear of him and began to fondle his knobbly head.

"More bark than dog," Marcia confirmed with a chuckle. "Likes his belly rubbed, too. Mind you, he's not daft. Wouldn't bide to his first home. Kept escapin' back here. That's how I come to call him Houdini. Can't keep him anywhere he don't want to be, an' that's a fact!"

A distinctive, rank odour eminated from the hound. Nicky's nose wrinkled. She sneezed.

"Hen muck," Marcia enlightened cheerfully. "Can't stop him rollin" in the poultry shed. Still, dogs will be dogs!"

She shrugged philosophically and handed Nicky a steaming blue mug with 'peace' written across it. A generous plateful of apple pie was placed on the table, with a warning to watch the thieving hound. Marcia then dropped into a chair and took up her tea, which she drank scalding hot with fierce concentration.

There was a small silence. Nicky sipped her tea.

"Got any other pets, Nicky, apart from that pony?" enquired Marcia abruptly.

Nicky said a regretful no. "Mum always wanted a dog, but now we've come to live here and the house is all. . ." she paused, feeling a stab of guilt.

"Posh?" suggested Marcia.

Nicky met a look that was wholly sympathetic. Putting down her tea, she drew a long breath and began to pour out her troubles. The move, her father's demanding new job and the sorrow of seeing so little of him, her mother's obsession with the house. . . even the fact that she hadn't taken to Chantley. She skirted round the pony, thinking the less said about Comet the better, but the rest—well, it was a relief to put it into words.

Marcia listened in silence, those impenetrable eyes watchful over the rim of her mug. When Nicky came to a halting finish, Marcia's face creased up thoughtfully.

"You know, I reckon once your ma's finished her homemaking, things'll sort themselves out," she said. "And Chantley ain't such a bad place. You just got to get used to it, Nicky."

Nicky sighed. Deep down she felt that if ever she did happen to come to terms with these shuttered valleys and secretive stretches of forest, part of her would always long for the freedom of the uplands and the sound of the little trickling becks. She saw Marcia's eyes deepen, and knew with utmost certainty that her thoughts were noted and understood.

Nicky swallowed hard. No one had ever read her mind like that before. In sudden agitation she began to babble wildly. "Mum. . . Mum's interested in conservation too, you know. She watches all the wildlife programmes on television and. . . and only last night she and Dad had a real ding-dong about whether a squirrel in the garden was a red or a grey. Dad said there aren't any red ones left, as the greys have taken over the reds' natural habitat, but Mum insisted it was a red by its tufted ears and bushy tail. And its colour, of course." She stopped for breath, the flush on her cheeks not entirely due to the heat from the fire.

"Your ma were right," Marcia said calmly. "We got colonies o' red squirrels in the forest. Seen that little fella in my yard?"

Nicky nodded. "I saw the badger too," she said shakily, and then blurted, "Oh, I WISH I could have her as a pet. But I suppose she's better turned free, once she's well again?"

Marcia was quick to agree. "Got a terrible torn leg, that sow. Had a fawn brought in same day, but it died." She heaved a sigh. "You can't win 'em all, Nicky."

"I suppose not." Marcia looked so dejected that Nicky felt a rush of sympathy and quickly changed the subject. "Zak dosed me with your headache medicine. It worked fine. Nothing Mum bought could touch it."

The dresser shelf with its bottles and jars was shot a satisfied glance. "Ah well, Nicky, that headache remedy's special," Marcia said. "It's one me gran'ma taught me, made from roots an' such. Gran'ma were a Romany AN' a seventh child! She KNEW things!"

The tabby cat chose that moment to uncurl herself and leap down. Moving lithely despite her bulk, she came to sit beside the fire and proceeded to wash herself. Contended purrs rumbled from her throat. Tutting indulgently, Marcia bent to stroke her. "Eh, more kittens! Like one, Nicky?"

"I would," Nicky said, "but Mum isn't keen on cats."

"Ah, that puts the tin lid on that little idea then, don't it?" Chuckling, Marcia gave her gingery head a shake. "I dunno, what with all these animals and me spinnin', sewin' and pottery, half the time I'm not sure if I'm on me head or me heels, an' that's a fact!"

"Doesn't Zak help with the animals?" Nicky asked, picking up her tea again.

"Prefer's his 'osses, does Zak," Marcia replied. She shrugged resignedly. "S'pose he copes fine, considering his handicap."

Nicky stared, mug halfway to her mouth.

Marcia enlightened her. "Zak's deaf," she said. "Took a bad dose a measles as a nipper and that's how it left him. He lip-reads something wonderful. And it don't hold him back. No one pulls a fast one over him at them auctions."

Deaf. Nicky put down her tea heavily. That explained Zak's concentrated stare and his harsh, unemphatic voice, his failure to answer when his back was turned. . . even his solitariness. All the little pieces fell into place. Not knowing quite what to say, she reached for her apple pie, and found it gone. Beside her, Houdini licked his whiskers with relish. Marcia gave a shriek of laughter. "Told you that dog were a born thief! Here, have another slice, then I'll show you me menagerie. . ."

Before long Nicky had been introduced to every bird and beast on the place. She was also given the low-down on their ailments.

The hedgehogs had apparently come to Marcia half-dead from dehydration. "Folk will insist on putting out bread and milk for them," she said exasperatedly. "Hedgehogs can't digest the lactose in cows' milk, you know. It scours them something dreadful. Goats' milk is better."

The birds were victims of domestic cats. People had rescued them and brought them for Marcia to heal. Usually it was a matter of waiting for their flight feathers to grown before they could be freed. The fox was a road casualty. "Had a broken leg. Often it's a simple case of concussion with road accidents. Badgers, hares an' fox cubs are for ever being' dumped on me doorstep."

"You mean people leave them and go?" Nicky cried in disbelief.

"O' course! Folk don't care to stick around here!"

"But... why ever not?"

"I dunno I'm sure!" Marcia sniffed derisively. "S'pose they're scared I'd turn 'em away. They'd be lumbered then with some flea-ridden wild creature, wouldn't they?"

"And DO you ever turn an animal away?"

"Never!" Marcia was emphatic. "I does me best. Can't do no more, an' that's a fact!"

She handled each creature lovingly. They showed no fear, made no attempt to bite or peck, almost as if they were aware that Marcia was their friend. Nicky's favourite was still the badger, which she was now thrilled to stroke.

The badger's outer coat felt coarse and oily, to keep off the wet, Marcia said. The undercoat was soft and dense, for warmth. She pointed out the strong forepaws, outward-turned for digging, and showed the pointed, yellowed teeth, with a warning that these could nip off a finger. The badger seemed to enjoy the fuss and attention. Not good, Marcia fretted, as it would have to fend for itself once returned to the wild.

Lastly Marcia invited Nicky into her pottery shed. This contained a kiln, a potter's wheel and a workbench. The air was stringent with the smell of clay, turps and paint. On a broad shelf, several elegantly shaped, unglazed vases awaited firing.

"You got to let your pot dry thoroughly afore you put it in the kiln," Marcia explained. "Otherwise you get a blow-out. Once your pot's ready, you biscuit fire it; that's like a slow cooking, see, to get rid of the last bit of moisture. This mustn't be rushed. You need a deal of patience—but that applies to everything that matters, don't it, Nicky?"

Nicky seconded that. "I can spend DAYS on a single drawing," she said. "I like it to be as perfect as I can make it."

"Ah!" Marcia's look was approving. "An artist!"

Nicky flushed. And then a brilliant idea struck her. Whilst showing her round, Marcia had admitted to running the rescue centre on the proceeds of her tee-shirts and pottery. This covered the cost of animal feed and bedding, but did not leave much over for sundries, such as bandages and basic oils for her remedies. Nicky was tempted to try a few wildlife sketches and offer them to Marcia for possible sale. Pen and ink drawings would be popular, she thought. Water colours might fetch more money. She made her suggestion cautiously.

Marcia was ecstatic. If Nicky liked, she could begin right now with a drawing of the sow badger. "I'll have to be getting off to me little job at the school, but you stay as long as you want, Nicky. Zak'll be home shortly. He's out on an 'oss he bought from an auction a couple of days back. He says some nutter's ruined it. But no doubt Zak'll sort it out, one way or another."

Nicky went a bright and glowing crimson, but fortunately Marcia was making for the house, muttering something about paper and pens. She was soon back with felt-tips and a dog-eared but quality sketchpad which, she said proudly, she had gleaned from a jumble sale.

"Be OK, won't you Nicky? If Zak don't come, don't worry about locking up. Houdini'll guard the place!"

Nicky watched Marcia stomp away over the cobbles, the wellies having been exchanged for a pair of pink trainers. Gathering her materials, Nicky returned to the badger and squatted down to study her: the bulky body and bushed tail, the way the ears tufted at the tips, the shadings of silver and grey in the coat. Eagerly she opened the pack of felt-tips.

So engrossed was she that the clatter of hooves did not register, and Zak had stabled Comet and discovered Cobber, still munching hay in the shed, before Nicky was even aware of the presence. The sound of her name being roared in no pleasant manner brought her startled to her feet, pens and papers scattering.

"So there you are!" Zak cried, bearin down on her in cold fury. "What you skulking here for?"

"I. . .I am NOT skulking," Nicky protested. "I was drawing."

"Drawing!" Zak sneered. He crooked a thumb towards the pony shed. "Why ain't you groomed my Cobber? Poor thing's sticky with dried sweat. Ain't nobody told you 'osses need looking after?"

Nicky blinked. "It got late. There wasn't time—"

"You got to MAKE time for your 'oss!" Zak growled. "Now get yourself over to the tap an' wash him down proper."

"I'm s. . . sorry," Nicky stammered. "I just didn't think."

"That's half your trouble!" Zak shook his head angrily. "An' I'm tellin' you this. If you neglect my Cobber again, you can have that other heap a mischief back in his place. Break your silly neck on him for all I care. Now scoot!"

Nicky set to work feverishly, hosing and soaping. Zak after flinging a box of grooming tools at her feet, perched himself on the tail-end of the flat-cart and watched her sourly.

"How d'you make out at the rally, then?" he enquired after a lengthy silence.

Nicky raised her head. "Cobber behaved exactly as you'd promised," she replied truthfully. Aware of Zak's eyes reading her words, she related Pru's plans for a Prince Philip team. "It sounds OK," she finished. "Pru said Cobber was a MADE gymkhana pony!"

A glimmer of amusement crossed Zak's face. "Didn't forget what I told you about tying him, did you?"

"Of course not!" Nicky frowned. "Things got quite iffy at times, though. Mum harped on about how much Comet had improved."

Zak gave a snigger.

"And Mrs Parks-Harrison went over the top—how good Cobber was, how clever we'd been to find such a perfect pony—"

"I told you my Cobber'd do all you asked," Zak cut in smugly. "Better than that heap o' mischief your ma bought you!"

At this Nicky pointed an accusing finger. "You told Marcia a fib."

"What me?" Zak cried in all innocence. "Who says I fib?"

"I do!" Nicky said icily. "You told Marcia you'd bought Comet from an auction. That was a whopper for a start."

Zak gave an eloquent shrug.

"You should be ashamed," Nicky said.

"Well I ain't!" Zak muttered flatly. "Trading 'osses is lucrative so Gran don't ask questions. You gonna finish grooming my Cobber today or tomorra, cos I'm getting corns on me backside sitting here!"

"You," Nicky snorted, "are incorrigible!"

"Gee thanks," Zak returned without rancour.

Finding herself smiling, Nicky selected a body brush and began to brush Cobber down. As she worked the banked clouds parted and the sun appeared, gilding the crumbling stonework of the lodge and hotch-potch buildings with gold.

Zak stood up. "Fancy a ride?"

Nicky was dubious. "Er. . . do you mean in the forest?"

"Be best," Zak said. "Want to knock more sense into that crazy chestnut I got from my auction!"

Nicky tutted and resumed grooming. Zak eyed her gentle strokes with disgust. "You'd best put more effort into that, Nick. You scared the colour'll come off, or what?"

Comet was a pain at first. Zak sat him like a leech, never shifting from the deep, well-worn saddle, while the chestnut jinked and bucked and snatched at the bit; a snaffle, Nicky noted. Zak held the reins loosely, his face inscrutable, eyes fixed on the chestnut's tight-pricked ears.

They had ridden for about thirty minutes before Zak gave the faintest indication that he was tired of Comet's tricks. The pony fly-bucked, and was given a reproving thump on the neck. "GIVE OVER!" Zak yelled at the same time.

Comet snorted indignantly. His tail gave that warning flick. Here we go, Nicky quavered, with a rush of relief that it was Zak about to be unshipped and not herself. Zak, however, was ready. When the buck came he drove the chestnut on, and when Comet hurled himself forward in those extraordinary leg-thrashing bounds, Zak yanked him in a tight circle, pulling him up sharply.

The chestnut stood like a coiled spring, snorting, thrashing his tail, the epitome of injured pride. Nicky hurried Cobber to safety beneath the trees.

"Walk on!" Zak ordered Comet. His heels nudged, his hands coaxed, he whistled gently.

Blowing a gusty refusal, Comet began to back. Fearful sweat sprang dark on neck and flanks, his eyes grew mean. He squealed, lifting his fore hooves in threatening little rears.

"I said walk on!" Zak growled. And sitting firm, he fetched the pony a whack across the shoulder with the end of the rein.

That did it. In a spurt of fury Comet went up, raking the air with wickedly swift hooves—and it seemed to

Nicky that all hell broke loose. Zak let out a yell that sent her blood curdling in her veins.

"OK, YOU PIG!" he screamed. "IF YOU WANNA RUN, THEN RUN!" And with another bellow he slacked the reins and kicked hard.

Comet took off; thundering down the path and vanishing into the thickness of the trees, and all that was left was the sound of pounding hoofbeats, pulsing through the forest until that too, was gone.

Summer dust settled on leaf and grass. Nicky wondered whether to turn for home. She was in no doubt that Zak would be all right. He had looked untroubled, almost as if he were enjoying himself. She was still sitting, undecided, when her ears picked up the beat of hooves. It came closer, and to her astonishment Comet appeared, not at that hurling gallop but at a rhythmic, controlled canter. Zak was grinning; Comet had a resigned look in his eyes.

Zak pulled the chestnut up beside Cobber. "Goes like the very clappers, don't he?" the boy declared nonchalantly. "Should enter him for the Pony National. He'd win, odds on!"

They continued their ride. Zak drove Comet hard, not giving an inch and praising lavishly if and when the chestnut responded. Every now and again he would whistle, softly, and the pony's ears would come back, listening, as if the sound conveyed some special meaning to him. Nicky could not credit the change in the pony, and she said so.

"That's cos he knows who's boss," Zak said, and promptly switched his attention to Nicky's riding.

"You're too stiff," he told her. "My Cobber won't do

nothing bad. Sit deeper and move your hips with the motion of the 'oss. Go with him, like. Use your body to push him on. That's better, see his nose come in? Now keep contact without jabbing his mouth. There, he knows you've got him, see? Watch his ears, Nick. You can tell what an 'oss is thinking by his ears."

An hour later Nicky's muscles screamed for respite, but she knew that she had learned a lot, and not just about riding. Zak knew the forest intimately. He pointed out fox earths and a whole colony of badger setts where, he said, the little sow would eventually be released.

They followed a deer trail and came across the herd, browsing the rank grass of a clearing in quick, nervous snatches, fallow deer, with rich red hides and dappled haunches. The two riders watched quietly for some minutes, until Comet gave a snort of impatience.

Heads shot up. Noses twitched, and in one fluid rush of movement they had bounded away, and there was nothing but the great trees quivering their leaves and the deep, secret shadows of the forest.

"Let's go!" said Zak, swinging the chestnut for home.

They were met at the gate by a beaming Marcia, flapping a sheet of paper which she thrust under Zak's nose. Nicky recognized her drawing of the badger.

"Ain't it WONDERFUL?" Marcia cried. "You got rare talent, Nicky! That creature's practically trundling off the page."

Zak inspected the drawing in silence. A grudging admiration sneaked over his face. . . but then the paper was slapped into Nicky's hand. "Not bad," he conceded. "D'you draw 'osses as well?"

"Of course. Why?"

"No reason!" The scowl was back. "If I wanted a picture of an 'oss, I'd go to a proper artist, wouldn't I?"

It was as she had suspected, Nicky concluded as she rode home. No sooner you believed you were getting through to Zak, he changed. Not the sort of person one could rely upon. The thought made her decidedly uneasy.

SEVEN

After that day Nicky went often to Keeper's Lodge. Sometimes she wondered why she bothered, as her friendship with Zak was questionable. If he was not berating her over her abysmal riding, he was scoffing at her growing interest in Marcia's wildlife scheme. Yet some compelling force made her rise early, groom Cobber—never again would she forget that—and hack him to the edge of the forest, where Zak usually turned up on Comet.

It took longer than Zak had anticipated to sort Comet out reliably. At the start of each ride the young chestnut was his scatty self, indulging in all his tricks to ditch his rider and escape. But with Zak there WAS no escape; buck, plunge or rear, the boy sat like he was glued to the saddle, an expression of bored resignation on his face.

Reins lightly held, head up, body poised and ready, Zak would have done credit to Mrs Parks-Harrison's teaching, the only difference being that Zak made that peculiar whistling noise, softly through his teeth. Contact, he called it. Nicky privately believed it to be part of his special magic. Whatever, Comet listened for the sound, twisting back his ears and making breathy little snorts in reply.

"When he's more balanced I'll get him jumping," Zak said one day as they cut through the forest. It had rained in the night and the ponies' hooves stirred a pungent smell of dank earth and wet vegetation. "He's got a pop in him like a kangaroo. Reckon with the right jockey, this little 'oss'll get to the top."

"Quite possibly!" acknowledged Nicky sourly. "Just don't expect ME to jump him!"

Zak shot her a sideways glance. "I said with the RIGHT jockey, didn't I?"

He sniggered and Nicky stiffened. Any more remarks like that and she would turn back for Keeper's Lodge. She had promised Marcia another sketch—a cat with kittens this time. Marcia's tabby had produced five kittens, all of which were promised to good homes. Nicky would have loved one. She even tackled her mother about having one, but was given a firm refusal.

Mum wanted a dog. Now that the house was in order she had begun to venture out for walks, and she felt that a sparky little terrier or perhaps a spaniel—a country dog that would enjoy a good ramble—would be company. Nicky was thrilled at the prospect, and every night they scanned the newspaper ads for a suitable puppy. Dad went a step further and had their name put down on a Cairn Terrier breeder's waiting list. Dad had always hankered after a Cairn.

The ponies were stepping out sensibly, neck to neck. Zak turned to Nicky and offered, in one of his lightning changes of mood, "If you want, I'll show you how to jump. There ain't nothin' to it, once you've mastered the basic skill."

Nicky shook her head. "Thanks anyway, but I prefer gymkhana with Pru. I'm getting into it now. We did team games on Tuesday."

"What, kids' stuff like Aunt Sally an' Dressin' Up Race?" Zak's tone was scornful.

"It was good fun AND it got us riding bareback!" Nicky said hotly. "The Flynns' Exmoors were dreadful though, bucking all the time. Pru says it's the boys' fault because they can't be bothered to school their ponies properly."

"Huh!" Zak was disgusted. "How did my Cobber make out?"

"Absolutely fine. It's just races with food he jibs at. He's more interested in scoffing the apples or whatever. He even eats potatoes. I have a real tussle with him and Pru has to send Dobs for more. He doesn't half grumble."

Hooting laughter, Zak leaned over and patted the chestnut's neck. "Gannet!" he scolded indulgently. "Reckon you'll never change!"

Reaching a fork in the trail, Zak reined Comet in. "How about going on to the meadows?" he suggested. "Ain't been that way yet, have you?"

"Meadows?" Nicky was suspicious. "You're not intending to gallop, are you?"

"Course not!" Zak threw her a despairing glance. "I just thought it'd make a change for the 'osses. It's a nice ride"—his face darkened—"at least it was afore Nigel Gregory built his house there!"

Nicky looked up sharply. "If we're passing Gregory's

place," she said with growing interest, "We'll see if Felix has arrived."

Zak looked at her blankly. "Felix? Who the heck's he?"

"Nigel Gregory's son," Nicky told him, smugly, as it was rare for her to know something that Zak did not. "Nigel's divorced. Felix lives abroad with his mother, but he's coming over for a holiday. He's supposed to be a brilliant rider."

"Is that so?" Zak stared at her disbelievingly. "Where d'you get that gem of gossip?"

"From Annis Reed," Nicky confessed, flushing.

Zak gave a snort. "I might a known. She's a regular News-o'-the-World, ain't she?"

Nicky laughed and they nudged the ponies forward, taking the narrow track which, Zak said, would eventually bring them out on the far side of the forest. The ponies strode out eagerly, enjoying the difference in routine. Zak rode Comet with his usual grim concentration but Nicky's mind hopped busily from one thought to the next.

Privately Nicky considered Zak's definition of Annis rather apt. Rich gossip, griddled to a turn in her father's dim, smoky little forge, was her constant source of information. And Annis could be relied upon to pass this on.

Smithy Cottage, where beamed and cramped little rooms echoed to the chatter of small children, fascinated Nicky. Mum had been aghast at the idea of such a large family living in so tiny a home. But, as Annis pointed out, countless generations of blacksmithing Reeds had occupied The Smithy. Chantley folk were sticklers for tradition and it was unthinkable that they should move elsewhere.

It was due to Annis that Nicky's interest in mounted games had grown. Both girls aimed to be included in Pru's Prince Philip Team—or the PPP, as it was now affectionately known—and spent hours in the Reeds' field, inventing weird and wonderful gymkhana games to prevent ponies becoming bored with their training.

Perched in a row on the gate, the Tinies made noisy and appreciative onlookers. They were also infuriatingly constant in demanding pony rides. This irritated the girls to the extreme. The ponies, however, seemed to enjoy it, Tiffin being resigned, and Cobber because he could cadge a reward by raising a pleading forehoof the moment his plump little rider slid to the ground. This brought screams of delight from the children, and cost their mother a fortune in polo mints.

Annis was sceptical over Nicky's friendship with Zak. "Eccentric," was her opinion of the boy. "Thinks of nothing but horses. Marcia's eccentric, too, but in a nice way. She brings wild creatures into school to show us and Mr Roland has us writing about them. Poems and things. We draw them, as well—or try to! It's ace."

Trendy and bearded Mr Roland was the new headmaster. "He's not really accepted by Chantley people, yet," Annis said. "Everyone says that since Miss Crump retired the village school's gone downhill. It hasn't though, Mr Roland's just got different ideas. I like him."

Nicky nodded politely, but it was hard to show an interest in a school that she did not attend. "Do you know what happened to Zak's dad?" she asked.

Annis gave a shrug. "Only that he buzzed off when the estate changed hands. He didn't get on with Nigel

Gregory. He even fell out with the Parks-Harrisons, though it wasn't their fault they had to sell. They lost their money—investments or something."

Nicky nodded.

"Zak's dad was a gypsy. Thin, shifty-looking. Zak's like him in a way. I never knew his mum, she died when he was tiny. You know he's deaf?"

"Yes."

"He's had a rough time. Maybe that's the reason he's so disagreeable!" Annis had pulled a face.

Cobber remained a close-guarded secret, locked in a dark corner of Nicky's mind. She worried constantly about her mother finding out, and she was still inclined to stumble over his name. She was often tempted to confide in Annis, but something—Annis' inclination to gossip, perhaps!—always prevented her. Zak, when she once mentioned how guilty she felt, told her bluntly not to be so daft.

Zak had a constant turnover in his stable. His most recent acquisition was a wagonload of youngstock from a sale of Welsh ponies at Hereford. These were now turned out in his field, waiting to be broken.

Zak's method of breaking was unconventional, to say the least. Nicky recalled a wild, frightened-eyed dun colt which had erupted kicking, and with murder on its mind, into the grassy orchard. Zak had approached it stealthily, palm outstretched, setting the colt's startled gaze with his own hypnotic blue stare.

The creature had stood, snorting defiance, tail twitching, hoof at the ready.

And then the whistling had begun. Softly at first, but

persistently. Faintly puzzled, the dun had dropped its head to listen. This was what Zak had been waiting for. Grasping the tangled forelock firmly in both hands, he craned up and whistled louder, directly into the colt's ear.

Slowly, before Nicky's astonished gaze, the animal had sunk to its knees to collapse in stunned submission at Zak's feet. Colt and youth had remained motionless for quite some minutes, until Zak shouted, "UP!"

The colt had lumbered up, shaken itself and careered off round the orchard, only to return to Zak like a trusty veteran, shaking its head and reaching out to lip his palm. Zak had rewarded him with a rare titbit.

The next day the dun colt, wearing a snaffle bridle and saddle, was being long-reined. A week later Zak was riding him through the forest, whistling, whistling, until Nicky felt that the very air was spinning with the sound. It even haunted her dreams, and she would wake, hot and troubled, staring into the darkness, while outside moths thumped against the window and swarms of tiny pipistrelle bats flittered about the eves of the house.

Despite being occupied with Cobber, Nicky had been on several outings with her mother. Only yesterday they had visited Ludlow. The town had not been greystone and rainwashed like Appleby, but rather more gentle, with alleyways of timbered, sideways-leaning houses and interesting little shops as dark as caves. There was the castle, too. A troup of actors had been rehearsing for the pending Shakespeare festival and they had stopped to watch.

Best of all were the art galleries.

Recalling them, Nicky said impulsively. "You know

Zak, I really liked Ludlow. There was such a lot going on."

"Eh?" Zak turned to her blankly, and Nicky realized that he had not heard. When she repeated her words, however, Zak's look was cynical. "I hate the place," he muttered. "Towns ain't my scene—all that traffic an' hurry up!"

"Oh honestly!" Nicky was exasperated. "You surely don't intend staying here all your life, breaking and selling horses?"

"I can think a worse ways to make a living," Zak retorted.

They came from the gloom of the forest into lucid, watery sunshine, with the sky brightening by the minute. It was pleasantly warm and insects buzzed sleepily. The ponies picked their careful way down a steep track, which brought them to the valley floor. Here a deep gorge, the result of ancient mineworkings, had formed a natural lake. The banks were thickly fringed with sappy willows, their pale, slender branches trailing into the water. Swans cruised gracefully in and out, guarding their reedy nests with wings arched like sails.

Sun-pennies glinted on the rippling surface, and small waves lapped against a crumbling jetty. A rowing boat, moored beside it, bobbed invitingly.

The ponies were mounting the path that led around the lake when there came a sudden whiffling of air through flight feathers, and from the trees darted a flash of sapphire.

"A kingfisher!" breathed Nicky, reining in. "Oh, see those colours! That startling blue and the orangy streak on its head!"

Even as they watched, the bird swooped and dipped into the water, surfacing with a thrashing, silver fish clutched tightly in its beak. As quick as light it skimmed off, back to its twiggy home, leaving behind a rippling catspaw that grew and grew and finally washed itself away.

"I'm coming back here with my sketching things," Nicky said. "Cobber stands while I draw, you know."

Zak just grinned. He nudged Comet on. Dragging her gaze reluctantly from the water, Nicky followed him between the softly waving willows and out into wide, open meadowland.

"Oh. . .!" gasped Nicky, blinking. She turned her astonished gaze on Zak. "You never told me it was anything like this!"

Zak's grin broadened. "Thought it'd surprise you. Ace, ain't it?"

Before them, acre upon acre of flower-strewn grazings rolled like some vast, multi-coloured sea towards a gorse-covered heath. Poppies grew everywhere, flares of defiant scarlet amongst the forests of meadowsweet and ranks of field spurge. Nicky, who prided herself on knowing the varieties of wild flowers, picked out loosestrife, melilot, thyme and bergamot, wild rue, hyssop. . . she could have gone on for ever.

The ground swarmed with butterflies—blues, fritillaries and marbled whites. High above a kestrel hovered. The vivid song of larks filled the air, welling up from a distance that was too dazzling to gaze into.

"C'mon," said Zak. Together they rode across the wilderness, the ponies' hooves swishing through beds of buttercups and vetches, scattering the loose petals which clung to their wet fetlocks in specks of gold and purple. The scent of crushed herbs was overpowering, and made Nicky's senses reel.

In the distance, enclosed by a rather ugly wall, loomed Nigel Gregory's redbrick house. The two riders approached it cautiously and, halting by the pillared entrance, peered in through the closed wrought-iron gates.

Wide lawns, unrelieved by flowerbed or shrubbery, flanked the straight, gravelled drive. The house was large and square—a no-nonsense sort of dwelling with dark-framed windows, a plain front door and a neatly-tiled roof innocent of chimneys. A row of garages and stables was fronted by a wide concrete yard. To the rear, Nicky caught a glimpse of paddock rails and thick grass.

"All terribly new-looking," was her opinion. "Not a bit like the Manor."

"Messed up the meadows somethin' dreadful, ain't it?" Zak muttered. Nicky nodded dismally.

The place was obviously deserted. "No Felix yet," Nicky said, craning. "Just look at those swish stables. Paddocks too. I can't see any horses, though."

"That's cos there ain't any," Zak growled.

"I suppose Felix'll borrow one, just for the holiday."

Zak shrugged, then began to twirl his whip thoughtfully. Nicky knew that action. Zak was on to something. She waited, but he did not enlighten her.

Comet twitched his tail, impatient of flies. Cobber had fallen into a light doze and Nicky let the reins go slack. Then the purr of an engine, speeding along the forest road, made her jerk up her head. "Someone's coming," she said. "Let's go."

They urged the ponies across the lane and into the cover of a belt of trees. Nicky had halted Cobber and Zak was having an argument with Comet, who had taken a sudden aversion to leafy shade, when bursting from the trees came Nigel Gregory's silver-grey saloon. It made a lurching stop at the entrance. As if by magic the automatic gates slid open, and the car whipped through and went roaring up the drive, its wheels spitting gravel in vicious little swirls.

The car stopped at the house and there was a lot slamming of doors, laughter and excited talking. A tall, powerful looking man with the gloss of good-living about him strode to the boot and yanked up the lid.

"Nigel Gregory!" Zak informed scathingly, having brought Comet round in a tight circle and forced him to stand. "The other'll be your Felix."

Felix was extremely suntanned, with the same dark brown hair as his father. He stood a moment, stretching and taking in his surroundings, then he sprang to help with the luggage. The two went into the house and the door closed, leaving the place as deserted looking as before—apart from the car, its silver-grey body glinting under the sun.

Zak eyed it with disgust. "Loada dog cans, cars! I can't be doin' with 'em!"

"Oh Zak!" Nicky faced him in amused disbelief. "That's the latest Porsche. Dad told me."

"I don't care what breed o' car it is!" Zak declared, tetchily but in a way that made Nicky want to laugh. "I'd sooner me 'oss 'n' cart any day! No petrol needed, so it don't pollute the atmosphere. Me gran'd say that's better for the environment and mebbe she's a point."

Nicky considered this. The North, swept clean by salt-laden west winds, whiffed faintly of the sea. Chantley was green-scented. Ludlow with its streams of traffic had smelled thick and oily. It was a sobering thought.

Zak's expression was guarded. His gaze swept the rippling pastureland rimmed with trees, the lake shimmering between its silver-willowed banks, and looking back at Nicky he said in a voice that was infinitely wise, "I guess for a lot a things, Nick, the old ways weren't all that bad."

Nicky met his look gravely and he grinned, not his usually sly or cynical smirk but a genuine smile, full of warm appraisal and friendliness. Nicky returned it and there was a small, perfect silence, into which came the sigh of the meadow breeze and the gurgle of some hidden stream. But then Comet began his impatient sidling, and Zak gathered the reins.

They rode the homeward path in a comfortable sense of companionship. It occurred to Nicky that she hankered less for her old home. She had grown to like the quiet little village, the snug valleys and the rolling meadows and cornfields. She had even developed a sneaking regard for the forest, with its mysterious trails and mossy reaches.

Chantley was taking hold.

"Gran's got a barn owl with a bust wing," Zak divulged suddenly. "She said if you've time, could you help her fix a splint on it."

"Why. . . of course!" Nicky felt a bubble of pure happiness explode inside her. This was not the first time that Marcia had called upon her assistance. Her artist's fingers, Marcia had declared, were ideal for performing delicate tasks. Unwittingly, Nicky was picking up many of the woman's skills. She was able to recognize the rarer plants that Marcia used in her remedies, and often gathered them for her during the rides.

As well, Marcia had begun instructing her in the art of potting. Nicky had not yet mastered the wheel; her pots tended to take all shapes, as though the clay had a life of its own. She was, however, skilled at design, and decorated a whole range of plates with flower or wildlife motifs. Marcia was so impressed with them that she had promptly put up her prices.

Zak darted a quick, embarrassed glance. "I've got a request too," he said hurriedly, a flush of red creeping up his neck. "Wouldn't mind a picture. S'pose you couldn't do me one?"

"Of course I will. What subject?" As if she couldn't guess.

"Do me Cobber, would you?"

"With or without white blaze and sock?" Nicky asked dryly.

"Do him as my Cobber, else he'll resemble Comet, won't he?"

"Not really," Nicky's tone was pure acid. "If I were to waste good paint on HIM, I'd do him breathing fire, with sparks coming from his hooves!"

Zak burst out laughing. "Just you wait, Nick," he said, urging the chestnut into a trot. "When I've done with this little 'oss he'll be a winner!"

Somehow, morning slipped into afternoon, what with helping Marcia set the owl's wing and then attending to the badger, whose damaged leg was mending swiftly.

Marcia said that this was due to frequent applications of comfrey poultices, and the addition of garlic and fenugreek to her diet of high-protein complete dog food. This Marcia acquired in bulk from the local mill.

"Be setting her free, soon," Marcia announced, securing the fresh bandage with a strip of plaster.

Nicky bit back a comment in defence of keeping the creature, and Marcia's eyes narrowed. "We might need the pen for some other poor beast," she pointed out gently.

Resigned but sorrowful, Nicky gathered together the soiled bandages. "Zak showed me the sett," she said. "I went back there and waited, but I didn't see any badgers."

Marcia sighed. "They're cautious creatures. Got to be. Had trouble with badger baiters last year…" She paused. "Badgers are a protected species now, see. But baiting still goes on, quiet like, in the dead of night. Folk get good money for badger pelts."

Nicky drew in her breath sharply. "How horrible," she said. "I HATE cruelty. I WISH I could stop it."

"Patience, Nicky." Marcia's voice was certain. "I reckon with your talent, anything's possible."

"You mean. . . through my drawing?" Nicky questioned uncertainly.

"Why not?" Marcia smiled. "You wield a lot a power there."

Nicky sighed. Marcia often talked in riddles. "I don't see what painting pictures has to do with saving animals from useless slaughter." She gave an impatient shrug.

Marcia smiled again and said surely, "There's different ways o' fighting, Nicky—different ways o' tackling most things, to be truthful! It makes a pattern, see. We're all of us part of it, weaving wonderful shapes with our comings an' goings."

Nicky strove desperately to understand and failed utterly.

"There's lots o' tangles, but not loose ends. Everything sorts out, in the end." Marcia stood up. "Come on, I need a hand feeding them baby hedgehogs. Then let's check that owl. He wasn't very perky, poor little Twoo. . ."

Nicky was thoughtful as she rode Cobber home. It was early evening and shadows were long-drawn across the forest trail. Somewhere, beneath Cobber's hooves, the badger families were stirring. All night long the forest throbbed with a special life of its own.

Was that part of Marcia's pattern, too?

None the wiser, Nicky turned Cobber on to the lane. He broke into a jog, keen to be home. Soon his hooves were scrunching up the drive.

"Dinner's almost ready," Mum called from the kitchen window. "Dad's in early for once. We can eat together, won't that be nice?"

Guiltily Nicky recalled her half-promise to go for a walk with her mother that afternoon. Occupied as she was at Keeper's Lodge, it had quite slipped her mind.

She turned Cobber out and tore indoors, anxious to wash and get out of her dusty clothes. Once the meal was over she intended to make a start on Zak's picture with a few preliminary sketches. She would paint it in water colours, she had already decided.

She would need quality paper; decent paints. Artists' colours were best, as opposed to students'. Good thing Dad was home, she could tackle him. At least now that they were better off, she did not have to wait until birthdays and Christmas for her art materials.

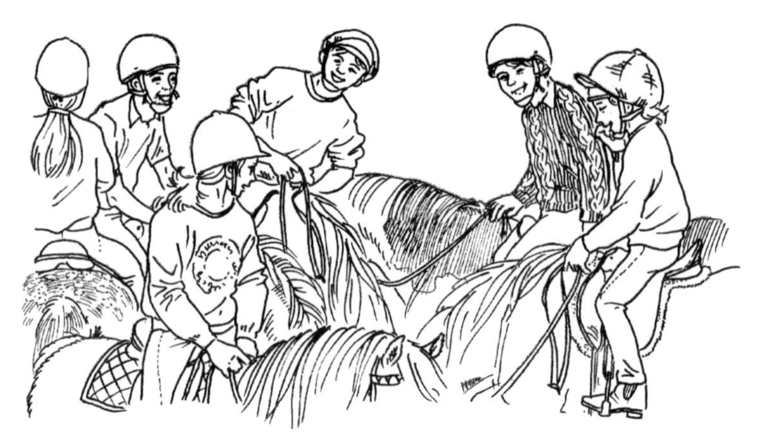

EIGHT

August came in with intolerable heat. Fields and meadowland were soon scorched to tinder under the blistering sun, and people were fearful of fire. The forest seemed to be holding its breath, as if the great trees knew that any movement might shed them of their thirsting foliage and bring it prematurely to the ground.

All the little gurgling streams had dried; even the river was reduced to a sludgy trickle. The level of the lake dropped alarmingly, and the swans' nests thrust from the muddy shallows like a row of tribal houses on stilts.

Everything craved moisture, from heath to farmland, where waves of golden corn rustled before the hot breath of the wind.

Nicky took to exercising Cobber at first light. It was actually Zak's idea—in fact he stoutly refused to ride ponies in the baking sun, when the multitudes of forest insects drove them to distraction. But then it was fine for him, as he never seemed to go to bed anyway, usually flopping down in the straw beside his precious horses and taking a nap whenever he felt inclined.

At first, it had seemed to Nicky like rising in the middle of the night. Once she was up, though, she enjoyed these early rides. Larks swooped and sang in the pearly bowl of the sky and Cobber's hooves echoed hollowly along the deserted lanes.

Zak was not always waiting at their place in the forest, as he was busy with his youngstock. Unperturbed, Nicky would ride on to the village, where Annis was usually saddling Tiffin.

The pre-dawn rising caught on. Often Annis and Nicky met up with Roger and the Flynns, and the five of them would go for long hacks across the heath, where a coolish breeze whispered. Nicky loved the heath, which sprouted heather and wild mountain thyme and was reminiscent of her well-remembered fells. Sometimes during these jaunts she fancied she caught the sound of Zak's whistling, flung into the air by the teasing summer wind. But when she strained her ears there was nothing. . . nothing but the hum of insects in the yellowing grass and the plaintive cry of a curlew.

One morning, all PPP members gathered for a ride. They set off at a brisk trot, with Dinah Mite's short legs striving valiantly to keep up with the bigger ponies. Lisa Scott was supposed to have come, but had failed to turn up.

"She's likely afraid Moonspinner'll damage his legs or something," Daniel said with a snigger.

Roger turned on him reproachfully. "Come on! It's not Lisa's fault she lumbered with a thoroughbred."

"Well, she gives me the pip, with her mincy face and stuck-up pony," Daniel muttered. "I can't think why she doesn't stick to showing, it's more her scene. She'll never make the PPP with that scrawny black."

"I think Moonspinner's beautiful," put in Mo dreamily. "I'd give anything for a pony like him."

"Then I guess you'll have to marry well, like Mrs Scott," Roger teased her good-naturedly. "Some wealthy guy who'll keep you in hunters and perhaps a racer or two!"

Mo turned on him in horror. "What? And live in a crumbling family mansion like the Scotts'? No thanks, I couldn't stand the mice!"

Five pairs of eyes widened in utter perplexity. "Er, you did say mice?" enquired Annis in a curious but faint voice.

Mo nodded cheerfully. "Mum went to the Scott's once for afternoon tea. It was one of those charity things in aid of the church roof or something. You know, proper tea not tea-bags, served in best china, wafer-thin cucumber sandwiches, diddy portions of strawberries and cream, queen cakes. . ."

Everyone waited patiently for Mo to get to the point. She took her time, running the tip of her tongue experimentally over the new brace on her teeth, flipping her hand over Dinah Mite's mane. ". . . And those horrid little macaroon thing that taste like stale bread. . ." She paused, lips twitching.

"Go on," urged Daniel breathlessly.

"Well, there they all were, dressed in their finery and posing on the Scotts' antique sofas," continued Mo, slowly. "Little fingers sticking out and trying not to slurp their tea, when suddenly this mouse popped out from under Mrs Parks-Harrison's seat—"

There was an explosive burst of laughter. Startled

ponies danced and jinked and Tiffin, grabbing the chance to make up to Dinah Mite, began to huffle pleadingly into her furry ear. Punch and Snippet put in a couple of mischievous bucks, tipping their none-too-secure riders on to their necks. Dutchman pranced on the spot and Cobber stood, his eyes blinking in bewilderment.

Tom and Daniel struggled back into their saddles and ponies were kicked on and reined in. Roger, his sunburnt cheeks glistening with laughter tears, said, "Whatever happened next?"

Mo gave a delighted chortle. "Apparently the DC's terrified of mice—you can't imagine anything scaring her, can you? She leapt up screaming and jumped on to a table, clutching her skirt round her knees in case it ran up her—"

"KNICKERS!" yelled Tom. A fresh uproar set the ponies jiggling again and sent a flock of grazing sheep bounding away with bleats of alarm.

"Actually I was going to say legs," gasped Mo, wiping an eye.

"So what happened then?" This from Daniel.

Struggling for control, Mo eventually came up with, "Oh well by this time tea was slopped, strawberries scattered, the Siamese cat was lapping the cream. Mrs Scott, who'd kept her cool and was still sitting with teacup poised, calmly rang for Mrs Butts the daily and. . . and. . ." She began to cackle again.

"And?" pressed Roger.

"She came p. . .prepared," Mo spluttered, "bearing TWO mouse-traps set up with best Stilton cheese! Mrs P-H was so crazed at the p. . .prospect of more mice she jumped off the table and ran out. Over the terrace and across the lawns, with the family beagles after her in full cry. She didn't half put on a spurt when one of them took a nip. Mum said she'd have won a gold speed medal."

This was more than anyone could bear. Ribald laughter held them in convulsions. Reins slithered through nerveless fingers as the riders fell helpless upon their ponies necks, and the heath rang with shriek after shriek of mirth. The ponies, now resigned, dropped their heads and began to tear determinedly at the dry, sheep-bitten grass.

"Oh my," moaned Annis, clutching her paining ribs with one hand and striving to drag Tiffin's head up with the other. "Dad never told me that one. And Dobs MUST have known."

"But did they catch the mouse?" Tom wanted to know, giving Snippet's rein a yank and shoving his toes back into the stirrups.

"Not sure," Mo chortled. "Mum couldn't escape fast enough. She was dying to laugh and didn't want to offend Mrs Scott. I do think the Siamese cat was pretty useless," she added more soberly. "OUR moggie'd have that mouse for breakfast!"

"Ace dog, though," Daniel put in. "I wonder what part of the DC he bit? I wonder if it's left a scar? I wonder—"

"If the poor dog got food poisoning?" joined in Tom. "Reckon a mouthful of Mrs P-H'd put any dog off meat for life!"

For the remainder of the ride each face wore a wide grin, and every now and again one of them would choke on a spurt of laughter. Daniel and Tom schemed endless mouse tricks to play on the DC. Roger invented a mouse-orientated mounted game. Nicky felt that she would never be able to look Mrs Scott in the face again.

Riding home, they met Zak on his flat-cart, a different vanner between the shafts—at least Nicky THOUGHT it was different. It was black, with precious little fringing to its fetlocks. It did though, have the same Roman nose and evil eye as the coloured, and was of similar height.

Zak whipped the horse on without casting the group a glance.

Nicky was baffled. "Why IS he so ignorant?" she muttered to Annis, who merely shrugged and said what did she expect?

The next rally was held on one of those sultry days when everything is bathed in dreary yellowish light, and flies swarm in their pestering thousands.

Felix Gregory turned up to watch, but not in riding gear. Mrs Parks-Harrison introduced him briskly and then left him to his own devices. After watching the mounted games briefly, Felix settled himself with Dobs' group to take in the working-hunter jumping. Nicky promptly forgot about him.

As the morning progressed, everyone became too hot and wearied to take much interest in work. Ponies stamped and flicked their tails at the flies. Children whined. Tempers became frayed. The Dragon seemed bossier than ever; had the Flynns played one of their mouse pranks on her, it would have been at their own peril!

Even Pru was mildly out of sorts. "Abstracted almost," Annis commented when they stopped for a breather, She lay flat out on the ground, fanning a sweat-slick face with her hand. It was actually lunchtime, but it was too hot to eat.

Nicky frowned over her sketchpad. As her mother was deep in conversation with the DC, she had left Cobber in the trailer, grabbed her drawing things and opted to sit with the Reeds.

"If that tape-player hadn't jammed we'd still be circling," Annis grumbled on. "Pru wasn't attending in the musical sacks."

"Good thing the DC didn't notice her," Nicky said absently. "She'd have ticked her off for lack of concentration!"

"CONCENTRATION! CONCENTRATION!" shouted a quick Tiny.

'Shush!" her mother admonished, darting an anxious glance. "Someone might hear."

"Who might?" asked the second inquisitively.

"I know, I know," piped the first. "It's Marcia the witchwoman!" Nicky's head shot up.

"WITCH WOMAN WITCH WOMAN, MARCIA THE WITCH WOMAN!" chanted the two. And regardless of the heat they joined hands and began to prance around in a lively dance. The third Tiny's face puckered and her lower lip began to tremble.

"Now you've frightened Andrea," their mother scolded, scooping up the child and distracting her with a sweet, pulled from her pocket. "I've told you many times there's no such thing as a witch, not here nor anywhere. Witches only live in story books."

"Can they escape?" Tiny Two questioned.

"Of course not, silly," reproved Tiny One, hopping up and down. Turning anguished eyes on her mother she announced shrilly that she was bursting for the loo. With a sigh Mrs Reed heaved herself to her feet and, herding all three together, hauled them away in the direction of the Manor.

"Here's to five minutes peace!" Annis said, rolling on to her stomach.

"Why do your sisters think Marcia's a witch?" Nicky asked crossly.

"Because she's an oddity, living in the forest with her animals and brewing up herbal cures," said Annis. "I would have thought it was obvious!"

Nicky shrugged and returned to her drawing and Annis, craning to look, gave a gasp. "It's the Manor! Gosh, that's REALLY good!"

Nicky held the picture at arms' length and squinted at it critically. "It's just a sketch," she said. "I'm doing a painting for Zak and I want the house as a background. I MUST get it right because I bet Zak knows every stone and crossbeam of the place."

"Well I hope he appreciates it," said Annis tartly. She was staring past Nicky now, down the line of parked vehicles. "I'd love to know what the DC's yacking about. She looks deadly serious. So does your mother."

"Oh," Nicky waved her sketchpad dismissively. "Probably something frightfully important, like what to wear for mounted games or whatever."

The day wore on. Uncomfortably sticky, the riders jumped and schooled. Pru, who seemed the only one untouched by the heat, had perked up now and worked the group fiendishly.

The Flynn twins came in for a lot of stick; Daniel for not attending, and Tom, who always had trouble stopping Snippet, for failing to try and school him. Lisa Scott came under fire for not riding determinedly enough. Nicky felt quite sorry for Lisa, as Moonspinner really was being a pig.

"Your jitters are going down the reins," Pru admonished, after the black had thrown up his head and fetched his rider a thwack across the face.

"Can't helb it!" Lisa gasped thickly, her hand on her throbbing nose. "I don't think Boonspinner's cut out for this. He gets too hotted up!"

"Glad you've found that out at last," Daniel said in a mutter.

"No one asked YOUR opinion!" Pru squashed him. Turning back to Lisa, she examined the girl's face, pronounced it sound and said despairingly, "How many times do I have to say that if you stop giving your pony heating feed, he'd be more manageable?"

"But it's by buther," Lisa wailed. "I'b bost awfully s. . .sorry b. . .but she keebs giving hib oats." She was darted a look of reproof.

"I've also stressed that you should do your pony yourself. Moonspinner's got a lot going for him. He's intelligent and speedy. There are worse ponies, you know."

Meaning mine I suppose," sighed Mo dolefully.

Pru sent an encouraging smile. "No actually, I didn't mean anything of the kind. Now. . ." she glanced around and said hopefully, "all set to try again?"

They tried, battling through a Postman Race and going on to an Apple Race. But even the ponies were out of sorts and made many mistakes.

You've got to shift yourselves," Pru chivvied. "Your ponies just aren't responding—" She broke off, glaring at Daniel who appeared to be contemplating something important in the sky. "Daniel Scott!" she cried. "Are you listening to me?"

"Sort of!" Daniel replied absently. "But my brain isn't really under control today."

"Is it ever?" wailed Pru. Heaving a sigh, she continued her tirade. "If you each do twenty minutes' circling and figure-eights per day, it will make your pony responsive. Do some vaulting on, and neck-reining. Get your pony interested. See?"

Damp, pale faces struggled to show enthusiasm.

"Assuming we make a team, we're going to have to work ALL winter, so anyone wanting to hunt"—Pru flashed a warning glance—"forget it!"

"Any idea when the area competition is?" asked Daniel.

"Sixth of April," Pru informed. "The Zone is at the end of July. I suppose you all know when Wembley is?"

"October!" Roger put in promptly.

"Oh ace!" chirped Tom. "That means time off school."

Everyone perked up at that, until Pru reminded them tersely that if they didn't get on they'd never make it as far as Chantley Show, never mind anywhere else.

They tried a Potato Scramble. Tiffin, in an unusual bout of peevishness, tipped Annis neatly onto the sun-baked ground the minute she leaned over to aim her potato into the bucket. It was because he objected to the noise, she excused him.

"But your potato never even MADE the bucket," Pru seethed. "Better try at home. Practice. Get those Tinies picking up your stray shots!"

Moonspinner hated the flying potatoes. The black's quivering muscle and rolling eye reminded Nicky of Comet. He would NEVER have stood for it, not in a million years. Lisa was by now reduced to tears.

Pru drove them relentlessly, pausing only for the briefest of ginger beer breaks.

"PHEW! Lead me to the nearest iceberg!" Mrs Flynn begged, mopping a perspiring brow. Mrs Reed, who came prepared for all eventualities, replied that she was sorry, she was clean out of icebergs but would a flask of ice cubes do instead?

Mrs Flynn fell on it gratefully, and spent cooling minutes smoothing ice over her burning cheeks and forehead.

Soon Pru was spurring the team into her favourite Walk, Trot and Gallop, which she still maintained was the best game for learning control, and which the group found unfailingly tedius.

It was sweaty and gruelling work. The twins' ill-schooled little Exmoors refused to work, but jogged infuriatingly with their noses tucked in and their short necks arched. Cobber became terribly out of breath with all the galloping and Pru, giving an anxious glance, advised Nicky to let him rest.

Roger and Dutchman worked stoically. Roger's face was crimson under his black silk, and the piebald steamed gently. Unmoved by heat and recriminations were Mo and Dinah Mite. Both enjoyed the work immensely, and completed each game with quiet fortitude.

At last the rally came to a lathered and blowing conclusion. The scattered gear was wearily gathered in; ponies were boxed.

"Thank goodness!" exclaimed Annis. "I can't wait to get home!"

"Me too," Nicky agreed. "All I want is peace and quiet."

It was not to be.

That evening, Nicky's mother served the meal with a troubled frown. "I heard something quite disturbing today," she began, dishing out platefuls of ham and offering crisp green salad.

Nicky recalled the muttered conflab with the DC and braced herself for what was coming. But then her father asked for butter to garnish his jacket potatoes. This was fetched, with a warning to remember his cholesterol.

"But I like butter," Dad protested mildly, taking a lavish helping and eyeing his meal with relish. He cocked a teasing brow. "I know a chap who died of curiosity, waiting for a spicy bit of Pony Club gossip!"

Nicky pealed with laughter, but her mother sent him an accusing glare. "What do you know about Nigel Gregory's scheme for a new leisure park?" she demanded. "Here, at Chantley?"

There was a rare silence. The smile fled from Nicky's face. She glanced in horror from one parent to the other. Dad, looking totally nonplussed, dropped his knife and fork with a clatter.

"A leisure park in CHANTLEY?" he repeated, brows raised. "Where'd you hear that bit of scaremongering?"

"I told you, at the rally!" came the tight reply. "Mrs

Parks-Harrison was full of it. It's to go on the meadows. Imagine it, James! All of those awful roller coasters, ferris wheels and water chutes. Noise, crowds and confusion! It will be the end of Chantley as we know it—"

Dad raised a protesting hand. "This is pure fabrication! Nigel's said nothing to me!"

"Is there any reason why he should?" asked Mum spiritedly.

"Well yes, dammit, I WORK for the man!" Dad said. "I'm virtually his right hand. If he had any such scheme I'd be the first to know."

"Not necessarily. Permission has to be granted before the plans are submitted. You wouldn't come into it until then."

Dad ran exasperated fingers through his hair. "You don't really believe Nigel would want a leisure park here?" he protested. "Not right on his own doorstep?"

"To make another million, yes!" retorted Mum stoutly. "HE could always move out. It's the rest of us who'll suffer. Think how this property will fall in value with a monstrosity like that on the doorstep!"

At this, Mum was reminded gently that their living depended on such er. . . monstrosities. She began to toy with her food. Nobody had eaten a morsel.

"I'm sorry, James," she said at last. "I'm not against development. Some places, like reclaimed slum areas and such, might be enhanced by the building of a leisure park. But Chantley?" The question hovered in the close, troubled air.

Nicky had heard enough. She rose abruptly.

"Nicolette? You haven't touched your meal. . ." Her mother's exasperated wail followed her across the dining room and into the hall. Nicky yanked open the front door and slammed out.

The garden shimmered with heat. Flowers wilted forlornly, and the drenching scent of the frilled pink trellis roses hung on the still, evening air. Nicky tore across the parched lawn and came to a gasping halt beside the tall, dusty shrubs at the gate.

She stood for a moment, passing a trembling hand across her eyes. Chantley meadows, destroyed by one of Nigel Gregory's developments? She could not believe it. The thought of those sweeping grasslands disappearing for good beneath a heap of concrete was more than she could bear.

And what of the village? How would its one narrow street cope with the inevitable streams of snarling traffic? And the lanes? Riding ponies along them would be hazardous. There was Zak, too, who travelled them with his horse and flat-cart.

Nobody would want to live in Chantley any more They would all move away; Parks-Harrisons with their 'chasers, the hunt people, the pony families who attended the rallies. . . right down to Zak and his dealer's yard.

Nicky felt a huge, yawning emptiness open up inside her. She was still standing, squinting abstractedly at the lurid crimson and ochre sunset, when the urgent patter of feet on the lane made her spin round.

It was Annis. "You've heard?"

"Just. Mum's furious. Dad denies it."

"All day I've had this feeling something was wrong," Annis fumed. "What with the DC po-faced, and Pru sort of detached."

Nicky said, "That's what the lunchtime conflab was about. And I thought it was something trivial!"

"Everything will be spoiled!" Annis cried. "It won't be just the meadows. There'll be all the cars and coaches. Hateful!"

"I was just thinking about the traffic problem," said Nicky. "I don't see how the lanes will take it all."

"They'll be widened, of course!" Annis snapped. "All the hedges grubbed out. Trees felled. The whole place will be ruined, because as well as going to the leisure park, some people are sure to treat the rest of the area as a playground. You know, holding car rallies and treasure hunts out here, things like that!"

"That's what happened in North Wales. Even Dad thought it a bit much. Eventually the countryside seemed to disappear."

Annis nodded. "Farmers get fed up with people picnicking and trampling all over their crops and leaving gates open, so they sell off bits of land and sometimes their barns for housing. You know the sort—Superior Country Homes, all wall-to-wall fitments and no soul! Oh grief, I HATE that Nigel Gregory!"

"Me too," said Nicky. But Dad knew nothing of the scheme, a small voice reminded. Nicky ignored it and said distractedly, "D'you think Marcia's been told?"

"Marcia?" Annis shrugged. In the torrid light her face was drained of colour. She looked older, wiser. "Marcia knows things without telling. . . if you get my meaning?" She paused.

Nicky gave a nod and then sighed. "Zak's yard is sure to be affected. There's only a narrow belt of forest dividing Keeper's Lodge from Lower Meadow. They'd get all the din—"

"And the stink of burger bars."

"Not to mention litter flying everywhere." Nicky pulled a face.

"Hikers would use the keeper's track as a short cut."

There seemed no end to the problems. Annis met Nicky's gaze worriedly. "How 'bout going down to the Lodge?," she suggested. "Maybe Marcia can cook up a plan to stop it."

"Stop it?" Nicky laughed harshly. "You must be joking! Once a place is earmarked for development, that's that!"

The sun vanished behind the trees and the light subtly changed. Dark bastions of cloud were banking up in the west. There was the first mutter of thunder, and a sinister little wind fretted across the fields, stirring the shrivelled leaves of the shrubs. Nicky felt its hot whisper on her cheek.

"I don't suppose it'd do any harm to try Marcia," she said uncertainly.

Seconds later both girls had shot through the gateway and were racing sure-footed along the storm-deepening lane to the forest.

NINE

Marcia was outside, bedding down her animals for the night when Nicky and Annis stumbled into the yard. Houdini set up a frenetic barking and there was an indignant clucking and flapping of wings from the poultry house.

"Houdini, quiet!" hissed Marcia, inching forward and peering into the gathering gloom. Seeing the girls, she threw up her hands in surprise. "Why bless me, what you doing here with a storm gathering? Come inside. Me kettle's on, we'll have a brew!"

A witch's brew, Nicky thought a touch hysterically as she followed Marcia into the lodge. Houdini ran ahead of them, waving his rat-tail and wafting a pungent reek of hen manure. He went to lie on the hearth, which was already crowded with the mother tabby and kittens.

Zak was seated at the table, cleaning harness. Glancing up, he greeted them with a frowning nod.

He's in one of THOSE moods, was Nicky's first thought as she cleared a chair of Green leaflets and flopped down. Annis did likewise. Marcia lifted the hissing kettle from the hob and began to make tea. She seemed preoccupied and not at all her chatty self.

A dagger-gleam of lightning lit the room and Annis jumped. "Ugh, I HATE thunderstorms," she said in a high, scared voice.

Nicky, who considered the storm the least of her worries, began to relax in the familiar clutter of Marcia's home. The rattle of the biscuit tin brought Houdini's head up expectantly. Marcia handed out steaming mugs of tea, offered cookies—chocolate chip, Nicky's favourite—and settled herself in her chair, her small feet in their pink trainers planted firmly on the brass fender. She sipped tea, her expression remote in the flickering firelight. The tabby left her kittens in a tumbled pile on the hearthrug and leaped up on to Marcia's lap. Loud purrs soon rumbled into the room.

There was an awkward pause. Annis caught Nicky's eye and bit her lip. The closeness of thundery air combined with the warmth from the fire made the place unbearably hot. Nicky could scarcely breath. She really had no idea what they were doing here, with dusk coming on and a storm threatening. It had just seemed the right thing to do at the time.

Zak pushed the jumble of tack away and, resting his elbows on the table, fixed Nicky with a gloomy stare. "S'pse you two've hot-footed down here over this leisure park rumour?" he said. "It ain't half been a day, with one thing and another!"

"Oh?" Nicky shot a startled glance at Marcia. "What else has happened?"

Marcia's lively face crumpled. "It's me little job at the school," she said, gesturing towards the mantel where, propped against the clock, was an official-looking white envelope. "It's a letter saying Chantley Primary's going to be closed down."

Her voice was choked and quiet. The girls stared aghast,

"Chantley Primary? Closed?" echoed Annis. "But. . . but why?"

"Dunno, I'm sure." Cradling her mug in her hands, Marcia took several deep gulps of hot comforting tea. "It ain't as though the school's no good. I can't make out what them officials in the Education Offices are playin' at!"

"I bet it's because the numbers have dropped," Annis said. "Dad said the Shropshire Authorities were clamping down on village schools. He didn't mention Chantley, though. Fancy him not hearing!" She sounded quite affronted, and Zak darted her a shows-you-don't-know-everything look. Annis' face tightened.

Nicky let out a sharp breath. "Does the letter say when it's to close?"

"Next year," Marcia said.

"What will happen to the children?" asked Nicky.

"Reckon they'll be carted by bus to one of them big new primaries in town," Marcia said. "That's the usual move, ain't it?"

Annis gave a cry. "But that's not on! I'm due to leave next year anyway but our Mum will want the Tinies to go to school here in Chantley, same as herself and Dad, and Gran and Grandad Reed, and—"

"Methuselah and his aunty?" added Zak, sniggering.

Annis shot him a look of pure venom. "It's all right for you, Zak Shone," she said cuttingly. "YOU hardly ever went to school so you can't be expected to care about the place!"

Zak gave another of his exasperating sniggers and Annis looked even crosser. Marcia, wrapped in her troubles, shook her head worriedly. "I'll miss me wages something terrible," she fretted. "Don't know how I'll manage, I'm sure."

"Come on now, Gran. There's always the 'oss money," Zak reminded her with rough kindness. "And it ain't as though you got nothing to do all day. A thriving cottage industry your got here."

"But I enjoy me little job," Marcia protested. "It keeps me in touch with folk."

"Can't you kick up a fuss?" Nicky put in. "What does the headmaster say?"

"Mr Roland ain't here," Marcia replied dolefully. "Ain't seen him since we broke up. I dunno where he is."

"He's touring France," Annis announced, smugly, with a sidelong glance at Zak. "He goes every summer for the whole six weeks. Grief, he's in for a shock when he gets back!"

"Tough!" snarled Zak. "What d'you bet Roland knew about the school trouble all along and that's why he's buzzed off?"

Marcia gave her head a firm shake. "He wouldn't do that, not Mr Roland. Very considerate to his staff, he is." She sniffed sadly. "I were doing a fine job at the school in more ways than one. Them kids were converting nicely to a Green way o' thinking."

A rumble of distant thunder made them all glance up and Houdini began to pant. They could hear the wind, tossing the trees. It moaned its way around the yard, whined across the roof and whistled down the chimney. Smoke gusted into the room.

Annis made a frightened little sound in her throat. The tabby slithered from Marcia's lap and went to curl around her kittens. Marcia, who like Nicky cared not one jot about the storm, fixed her eyes on Annis and repeated sharply, "Ain't I done a good job with you kids? Do them lads go bird-nesting these days?"

Annis said haltingly not as far as she knew.

"Frog spawning? Rabbit trapping? Catching poor harmless little butterflies and sticking 'em in glass boxes?"

Annis's head shook wildly to all these misdeeds.

"Well, there you are then!" Marcia said roundly. "Got them kids to respect the place they live in, ain't I?"

Zak gave a snort like an impatient horse. "If this leisure park takes off, Chantley won't be WORTH living in! I ain't bothered about the school meself, but how'll I trade me 'osses with some great funfair sittin' in our back yard?"

Marcia let out a fierce breath. "If that ain't typical o' you, Zak Shone! Thinking o' nothing but 'osses!"

"It ain't just that," Zak rounded on his grandmother indignantly. "I don't take kindly to the place being ruined. Left to money-grabbin' fools such as Nigel Gregory, Chantley'll be like everywhere else. A flamin' mess!"

"Zak's right, I suppose," Annis admitted with some reluctance.

"What'd you say?" Zak turned to her scowling and Annis, blushing, was forced to repeat her words.

Zak gave a grunt and, snatching up a blinkered bridle, began to take it apart angrily, yanking at the buckles and flinging the pieces down on to the table. Marcia leaned back in her chair to finish her tea. She seemed totally drained. She still had expressed no feelings about the leisure park; it was as if all her worries were centred on the school. Annis nibbled on a biscuit.

Nicky eyed each one with concern and then cleared her throat. "Perhaps we should tackle one problem at a time," she declared reasonably. "When you think about it, no one's going to build a leisure park overnight. Plans have to be approved and that sort of red tape always takes ages. So why don't we shelve Nigel Gregory's scheme for now and concentrate on the school?"

She paused. Marcia was staring over the rim of her mug. Annis crunched the last of her biscuit. Zak unconsciously lowered the bridle to the table.

"Well come on," Nicky urged, drawing herself very upright in the chair. We can't sit back and watch some faceless authority take away our school, surely?"

"You're dead right, Nicky," Marcia agreed with a hint of her old spirit. Leaning forward, she grabbed the teapot and refilled her mug. "We got to think up some ideas!"

"Yes, but what?" Annis joined in dubiously.

The silence between them was long and absolute, while outside the summer storm edged closer. The wind stirred the curtains and rattled the letterbox. The fire crackled, the tabby purred and Houdini's rat-tail went swish, swish, swish in hopeful anticipation of biscuits. They all sipped tea and the silence ticked on.

Annis gave a tentative cough. "Er, I suppose we could

start with the PTA—"

"Oh, of course!" cried Nicky. "The PTA can get everyone to join forces and fight it."

"Huh, I don't think so," Annis said, her hand sketching a small gesture of defeat. "There's nobody all that riveting on the committee. Only the rector who's sweet but doddery, and a couple of farmers who are always busy with their livestock. Of course there's Mr Roland—"

"Yuk!" exclaimed Zak, and was thrown a crushing look from Marcia.

". . .And one or two mothers."

"Load o' jelly!" Zak growled. "You want someone with a bit o'a smack in 'em."

At this Annis gave a sudden squeal. "I almost forget, Mrs Parks-Harrison's on the committee, too!"

"BRILLIANT!" yelled Nicky, so loudly that Houdini gave up on the biscuits and scuttled for cover under the table. "If the DC can scare us—and let's face it, I've seen the twins, who are as hard-faced as they come, positively QUAKE at her voice—then she can put fear into the Education Officials too."

Annis nodded. "Mrs P-H does care about Chantley."

"She cares more for the Pony Club," Zak said in a mutter.

"Mebbe her just needs motivating," Marcia reasoned shrewdly.

And then something struck Nicky with such force that she gasped. "MUM!" she shouted wildly, waving her hands at the mystified faces before her. "Mum's the motivation! She's finished doing up the house and she's bored out of her mind. You should have heard her snapping at Dad over the leisure park, he could hardly get a word in! What's more, she's TREMENDOUS on a committee. Listen. . ." Her mother, she explained in a rush, possessed a flare for leadership. Bossy to the core, she got things moved while everyone else sat about staring at cobwebby ceilings or ruffling their notepads. She had actually established the PTA at Nicky's first primary, and was now firmly ensconced on the committee of Mountbank.

"She'll go to any lengths. She seems to know who to contact, and when. She's good at money-raising events, too. A parents' Bingo Evening once made hundreds of pounds, and a sponsored dog walk'—Nicky's eyes rolled—"brought in a positive fortune!"

Zak frowned thoughtfully. Marcia blinked.

"But. . . would your mother be interested in campaigning for Chantley School?" asked Annis. "Especially with you going to Mountbank?" Her cheeks went an embarrassed pink but Nicky's mind was set.

"I'll jolly well MAKE her interested!" she said determinedly.

A glimmer of hope sparkled in Marcia's eyes. Zak shrugged. Annis twirled a nervous smile.

Another clap of thunder sounded. The storm was closer.

"Marcia? Marcia Shone, do you mean?" Nicky's mother placed her cup and saucer on the pine kitchen table and sat back with a frown.

"That's right." Nicky's fists were tightly clenched in her lap. Far into the night, while the storm had rumbled and grumbled but failed to come to fruition, she had plotted and planned. If Mum did not think Marcia's plight worthy, then the idea was doomed.

But Nicky had misjudged her mother.

"That woman's extremely talented!" she said. "She makes her own pottery and sells it in Ludlow, doesn't she? Unusual vases, decorative plates and such?"

Nicky nodded. "And she's involved in wildlife rescue."

"So I believe. I heard her holding forth in the village shop one day last week, on Green issues. There seemed nothing she didn't know. She really got me thinking!"

"She would!" Nicky agreed swiftly. "And Mum, as well as doing her animals and pottery, Marcia goes out to work."

"Oh?"

"At the village school."

"She's a teacher?"

"Not exactly. . ." Nicky hesitated, took a deep breath and plunged on. "Marcia's the caretaker, but she does other things like taking wild animals for the children to see and telling them how to care about the countryside. And now the school's to be closed she'll be out of a job, and she won't be able to afford to keep—"

"The school's being WHAT?" The words were spoken slowly, but there was no mistaking the outrage in Mum's voice.

"Closed," Nicky gulped. "Apparently the numbers have dropped despite people like the Reeds who have triplets. The Authority's angling for closure. Marcia's really devastated."

"I'm not surprised!" Mum drew herself up aggressively. "Why, apart from anything else the school is the heart of a rural community."

"Then why can't I go there instead of Mountbank?" demanded Nicky with a flicker of rebellion.

But Mum had reached for the local directory and was riffling through the pages. "I can guess who's on the PTA." She muttered abstractedly. "I believe the headmaster's holidaying in France, so we're unlikely to find him in a hurry! Then there's the rector, and that farmer at the lane end who involves himself in most village affairs—"

"Don't forget the DC!"

The telephone book dropped from Mum's fingers. "WHY, OF COURSE!" she cried. Their eyes met conspiratorially, and Mum gave a breathy little laugh. "Mrs P-H! The very person!"

Drawing a determined breath she grabbed the phone and punched out the number. Almost immediately the unmistakable tones of Mrs Parks-Harrison boomed into the room. Nicky quailed, but her mother smiled confidently. "Good afternoon, Karen McGuire here."

"Ah, Karen my dear gel. Awfully glad you rang. You'll never guess what's happened!" Mum made a wry little face as the DC launched into a stream of Pony Club woes. The gymkhana arrangements for the show were proving a perfect headache this year, what with the shortage of stewards and Major Crompton promising to judge and now saying he can't. ". . . You know the Major, of course?"

"Actually, no," said Mum.

"Awkward character. Most unreliable!" The DC gave a snort of derision and ploughed on. The jumps badly needed painting, and there was all that gymkhana equipment to overhaul, not to mention the working hunter obstacles. Dear old Dobs could hardly be expected to do everything, could he?

Nicky's mother said no, of course not, and with a calculating lift of her brow at Nicky, promptly offered her services.

Mrs Parks-Harrison breathed a gasp of surprise. "Oh, would you? Would you really? My DEAR gel, what CAN I say. . .?" Here thanks flowed, thick as treacle.

"You're very welcome!" Mum's eyes sparkled. "After all, we mothers are positive SLAVES to the Pony Club! I do, however, require a small favour in return. . ."

There was a powerful silence from the other end. Mum straightened her shoulders ever so slightly. Beyond her the window gave a view of troubled skies rolling with purplish clouds.

". . . It concerns the impending closure of Chantley Village Primary School," continued Mum. "It's only just come to my notice, and frankly I'm APPALLED that nothing is being done in protest!" Speaking briskly, she outlined the duties of the PTA, elected herself an interested party and finally demanded an emergency meeting.

"You. . .you mean now?" quavered the DC. Nicky could picture her, glancing at the grandfather clock in the Manor hall, where oak panelling was hung with grinning foxes' heads and a vast collection of hunting horns and whips.

"I don't feel we should dally," Mum prompted. "After all, it's a case of no school, no village. Once the community spirit dies, people move out. Cottages are snapped up as holiday homes—occupied for odd weeks in the year. Speaking for ourselves, we'd be unlikely to stay at

Chantley under those circumstances. I'm sure others would feel the same.

She paused dramatically, and then hammered her punch line home. "Just consider, then, what might happen to the Pony Club!"

There was a strangled gasp, as though the woman's flame was being extinguished. Nicky imagined a sorry little dragon creeping away into its cave. Mrs Parks-Harrison then began to stammer something about discussing the matter more fully, and could Karen be at the Manor within the hour?

"Of course," Mum agreed smoothly, and bidding goodbye she rang off. She had turned triumphantly to Nicky when there was an ear-splitting crack of thunder and the first heavy drops of rain lashed the window. Mum flicked an anxious glance. "I hope this storm keeps off until I get there. I could be some time; you'll be all right, won't you, Nicky?"

She'd got her name back!

Nicky grinned broadly. "I'll be fine," she assured "I'm going to start a painting. Dad bought me some watercolours from that terrific art shop in Ludlow."

"Oh really? How lovely. Tell Dad where I am, will you? And Nicky. . ."

Nicky grinned again. "Yes?"

"If I'm really late, d'you think you could rustle up a meal for us all? There's plenty in the freezer."

She whipped round and marched out. Nicky heard her quick footstep on the stair. A hasty change into battle dress and a swift application of warpaint and Mum would be ready for the fray! Nicky gave a satisfied chuckle. Once she had got her picture of Cobber with its background of Chantley Manor outlined in pencil, she would prepare sausage and chips and mushy peas for dinner, followed by dairy ice cream, strewn with nuts and oozing with chocolate sauce.

TEN

"I think your mother's a positive genius!"

It was the cool of the morning and the ponies plodded sleepily along the dew-damp lanes. Since leaving the forge, Annis had done nothing but sing Nicky's mother's praises.

"She's spurred everyone into action," Annis enthused, nudging Tiffin with her heels to wake him up. "People tend to do a lot of grumbling and leave it at that, but now. . ." she paused effectively.

Nicky threw a knowing look.

For the past two weeks the name Karen McGuire had been on everybody's lips. Following her discussion with Mrs Parks-Harrison, an emergency meeting had been called. The weather, which had threatened thunder for days, chose that afternoon to break. Driving her car through one of the worst summer storms on record, Karen had sallied into that meeting resolutely. Her speech was impressive, stirring even the most laid-back committee member with her spirit of staunch determination.

Ideas for saving the school were soon buzzing around the panelled hall of Chantley Manor. To a background of unseasonal hailstones, battering against the mullioned windows, a letter was composed objecting strongly to the threatened closure.

The wind increased. It roared across heath and meadow, flattening the corn, streamlining the paddock grass into fast-flowing current and striking the wattled wall of the house in frantic thumps and clouts. Lightning stabbed and drum-rolls of thunder echoed across the valley. It grew chill. Mrs Parks-Harrison had a fire lit in the vast open hearth and the smoke, gushing up the wide chimney, was caught by the wind and torn away in a swirling race over the ravaged orchards and gardens.

In the forest the great trees swayed and thrashed. Rotten branches fell victim to the fury, and the air was filled with flying leaves and twigs. Marcia, shawl over her head, scuttled around the yard shutting in the animals. In the village people battened down their windows and closed their doors and prepared to sit out the worst.

Oblivious to everything but the matter in hand, Nicky's mother hammered out their carefully-composed letter on Mrs P-H's vintage typewriter. Filled with enthusiasm, Mrs P-H then called a reluctant Dobs, who was already half-drowned from bringing in the horses, and requested him to deliver the letter by hand to Ludlow Education Offices.

Dripping copiously onto the faded Persian carpet, Dobs blinked at the DC as though she had taken leave of her senses. He even opened his mouth to argue, but caught Karen McGuire's steely eye and promptly shut it again. Resigned, he found himself revving the Land

Rover and negotiating lanes whitened and made unfamiliar by profuse drifts of hail.

The letter was handed in, but it was a pallid and shaken Dobs that returned home in time to attend to evening stables.

"It isn't as if the school's being shut down next week!" he complained to Pru, who had dashed out to help him. "They could have put their dratted letter in the post."

"Never mind," said Pru soothingly. "Consider it your part in aiding the Save Our School Campaign. For that is surely what it is!"

The storm abated at last, but the hot dry spell was well and truly broken. Several more meetings had taken place, during which Chantley steamed and bubbled under torrents of wild summer rain. Out from mothballs came waxed coats and wellies. Farmers battled across land knee-deep in mud and worse. Dobs kept his precious brood mares in. A rally had to be cancelled.

Marcia was overrun with half-drowned hedgehogs and baby rabbits. Village mothers strove desperately to occupy their bored children. The forge furnace was extinguished for the first time in years.

To top it all, the river flooded and burst its banks. Old timers watched the rising level with anticipation, their tongues wagging about an instance long ago when the village street became awash and people were forced to abandon their homes.

Nicky's mother swept along with her plans impervious to weather and gossip. Chantley Manor had almost become her second home. Then there had occurred a slight hiccup. Because she was not officially connected with Chantley Primary School in a parental capacity, some objection to her being in command was raised by one of the school governors.

Nothing daunted, Nicky's mother had promptly established a separate Save Our School Committee, electing herself as Chair and Mrs Parks-Harrison as Hon Sec, the latter being a formidable opponent in the face of trouble. Roger Davies's mother, sharpwitted and organizing, was on the board too. So, surprisingly, was Lisa Scott's. Each time the coolly elegant Mrs Scott called at The Briars though, Nicky recalled Mo Stephens and the mouse in the sofa, and had to make herself scarce in case she disgraced her mother by dissolving into fits of laughter.

Despite the threats hanging over Chantley, Nicky was never happier. Her mother was back to normal—well, almost. A change in fortune was bound to leave its mark. There was still the occasional jaunt to antique auctions, the odd splurge on new clothes, but this Nicky did not mind. It was great having the house filled with people. If Nicky wished to escape them she had only to go to the spare bedroom, which Mum had now skillfully converted into an art studio; north-facing window giving the best light, varnished floor, pin-boarding for completed works. Nicky could paint to her heart's content and no one ever disturbed her.

Public response to the campaign had been tremendous. To an open meeting, held of course at the school, people had poured in droves; not only from the village, but from outlying hamlets and isolated farmsteads. Past pupils, many now retired and filled with nostalgia for the old days, shuffled in alongside the enthusiastic young and the more reticent middle-aged. All were unanimous in the decision that no way would they allow their village school to be closed. In a three-hour discussion their campaign was plotted. They were prepared to go to any lengths, even as far as camping on site and forming a human chain around the school's solid Victorian walls.

Chantley buzzed with nothing else for days. James McGuire, relieved that his wife had something positive to occupy her, gave the campaign his complete support. Mr Roger Davies Senior, who ran his own computer software company, offered computer files of the minutes of each meeting, and produced copious print-outs so that everyone was kept up-to-date with progress.

Mr Scott, a wealthy landowner with two mixed farms to his family name plus the mice-ridden country mansion, invested a generous sum to be used as cash flow. This came in handy for sundries such as stationery, postage, advertising, not to mention the petrol expenses incurred by all the running around.

Meanwhile, the PTA were sending out other feelers. The local MP was urged to present the cause in higher places. A hotline had been sent across France to bring back the holidaying headmaster, but to date he had proved elusive. It was, as Mrs Parks-Harrison pointed out, rather like finding a needle in a haystack, France being an exceedingly LARGE country.

The press had wind of the anti-closure scheme and sent a reporter, who interviewed old and new pupils alike. A spectacular front-page spread, complete with photographs, appeared in the local paper. This prompted support from further afield.

"Marcia's quite perked up," Annis declared happily, checking Tiffin from snatching the roadside grass. "She's full of plans for the campaign."

Nicky said she knew.

Sizzling with ideas, Marcia issued a request for whatever old sheets and curtains people could spare. A little path had been worn alongside Zak's flatcart trail, where willing feet trod the way to Keeper's Lodge. The pile of jumble grew outside the gate. Houdini never seemed to stop barking. Mrs Parks-Harrison rootled round her attic and discovered an ancient hand sewing machine, which Dobs presented in immaculate working order to Marcia.

Marcia was ecstatic; this helped her workload considerably. The whirr of her frantic sewing could be heard far into the night as she churned out colourful banners, all boldly emblazoned with the words SAVE OUR SCHOOL.

A contact generously donated a range of tee-shirts, which Marcia hand-decorated with slogans. These were widely bought, and the proceeds ploughed back into the campaign.

Nicky's arm ached from painting vast posters, depicting the school building at its most attractive angle. The posters were distributed by a complaining Zak with his horse and cart, and were displayed at every crossroad and junction, tied to a tree or gate with lengths of baling string.

Zak alone remained impartial to the campaign.

"You should be ashamed," Nicky chided him when his grumblings began to get Marcia down. "Instead of objecting, why not help with the campaign?"

"What ME?" Zak let out a hoot of laughter. "Never attended school much, did I? Teachers never took to me. Said I was indifferent or worse. Half the time I couldn't hear what they were on about, an' the other half—well, mebbe me mind were on me 'osses!" Zak looked sheepish, but then his face tightened and his eyes became hard. "I'm more concerned over the leisure park. Let them start fellin' the forest an' diggin' the meadows, then I'll raise my objections, an' that, as me gran'd say, is a—"

"Fact?" finished Nicky tartly.

Zak grinned. "Let's say a promise!"

Joking apart, Nicky felt that Zak had a point. In their massive concentration on the school, the campaigners had totally dismissed the other problem, which loomed just as real and was a great threat to the continued life of the village.

There was also her own personal worry about Cobber. Guilt over the swap still gnawed at her. A few more weeks and autumn would be upon them and the pony would lose his summer coat. His new winter one would grow, warm and thick, and with it would appear that startling white blaze and sock.

At this point Nicky would resort to her original theory of tackling one problem at a time. Chantley leisure park was more pressing.

Nicky stopped Cobber from heading for the grass and darted a searching glance at Annis. "I know I'm jumping from one problem to another, but I don't suppose your Dad's heard any rumours about the leisure park development?"

Annis shook her head. "Not a trickle. But I did have an idea. Why don't we drop in at Chantley House to see Felix? Didn't he say at the last rally he'd welcome callers? I thought he sounded a bit lonely. And Nicky, when you think about it he's bound to know something of his father's plans. Once we're IN, we can quizz him—tactfully of course!"

Nicky assumed dismay. "You mean SPY? Why Annis Reed, I'm truly shocked!"

Annis flushed a guilty pink and Nicky cracked up laughing. "It's a BRILLIANT idea. I can't understand why I didn't think of it myself!"

"Most likely because I'm nosy and you're not!" Annis retorted.

A movement in the hedge caused both girls to glance up, and across the road slipped a vixen with three leggy, red-brown cubs in tow. Both ponies snorted. The girls stood in their stirrups to watch the quartet lope purposefully across the field and vanish into the cover of the forest.

"Soon be cubbing," Annis said. "Are you going on Comet?"

Nicky shrugged. To be quite honest she did not really care for hunting, though she had more tact than to mention this to Annis, and besides, "Didn't Pru say no hunting, as we'll be going all out for the PPP?" she reminded.

"Cubbing's different, and we don't know yet if there'll be a PPP," Annis pointed out. She laughed shakily. "Only two weeks to the show. Thank goodness for that storm. It's cooled things down no end AND got rid of those beastly flies."

"True. And the village didn't flood. I think those old gaffers who congregate on the green to smoke their pipes and chinwag were quite disappointed!"

Laughing, they rode on, with the sky lightening by the minute and the birds about their morning business. Mist hung in all the little hollows and the grass was fretted with cobwebs. The air was fresh, and the ponies, now wide awake, kept putting in happy little jogs as though they were pleased to be out.

"Did you ever paint that picture for Zak?" Annis enquired all of a sudden.

After a brief pause, Nicky said in a small voice, "Yes, a watercolour."

She had painted Cobber standing against a field gate, his dark eyes intent, his chestnut coat catching the sunlight. In the background was the timbered and mullioned face of Chantley Manor, with a suggestion of the stable-yard and horses' heads peering over half-doors. Clear skies, thronging with larks, met the distant forest in a lavender haze. The centre-distance showed the meadows, a riot of colour merging into the purple splash of heath.

The picture had all the essence of a languid August day, the sort to be stored in one's memory and cherished—Chantley at its most evocative.

"I bet Zak was dead chuffed," Nicky surfaced to hear Annis say.

Nicky's face tightened. "I wouldn't know. He wasn't in when I delievered it and I've not seen him since. He's been attending hunter auctions. And there was a Welsh Cob sale at Brecon."

"That was last week," Annis put her right. "D'you mean he's never even thanked you for the picture?"

Nicky shook her head. Actually she was wounded to the core by Zak's lack of response. It was like a slap in the face.

"Ignorant pig!" Annis was disgusted. "Mind you, it's only what you'd expect from the likes of him."

They came to a crossroads and took the high-banked, winding lane to the meadows. It was early yet, so the growl of an approaching vehicle surprised them.

"Drat! Why do they always come on the narrowest bit?" Annis cried, urging Tiffin into a fast trot.

Cobber followed. Over the clatter of hooves they could hear the car, speeding closer. Gaining an open gateway, they pulled the ponies in, Nicky battling a little with Cobber who thought he was going to the forest and objected to being swung in the opposite direction.

The car slipped past—long, low, silver-grey. They glimpsed a blur of faces and the flash of a hand raised in brief salute. And then the vehicle rounded the next bend and was gone. Clouds of dust, stirred by the wheels, settled on verge and tarmac.

Annis met Nicky's astonished gaze. "I don't BELIEVE it! That was Nigel Gregory! And did you see who was with him?"

Nicky gulped. Occupied with Cobber, she had seen only fleetingly, and she hoped she was mistaken.

"It was Pru, wasn't it?" she said, her heart sinking. "Pru Parks-Harrison, of all people!"

ELEVEN

"Pru's the very last person I'd expect to see in Nigel Gregory's car!" Annis exclaimed in dismay as she nudged Tiffin back onto the road. "And they looked so. . . well chummy! They were having a good laugh about something. Pru barely gave us a wave."

Nicky urged Cobber level with Tiffin. Suddenly she was weary of all the problems. She said, "Oh well, at least Gregory slowed down for the ponies."

"Only because Pru was with him," Annis said sharply. "He usually blasts along regardless. He almost took Tiffin's whiskers off one day, he was in such a tearing great hurry."

Nicky glanced at her watch. Not yet six. "It's heckish early. I wonder where they could be going?"

Annis shrugged. "I don't know as I care. In fact I've gone right off Pru Parks-Harrison! I bet her ma doesn't know she's out for a spin with HIM. Mrs P-H was awfully cut up when they had to sell the estate."

"But that wasn't Gregory's fault," Nicky pointed out with a hint of exasperation. "Being the present owner doesn't make him a criminal."

"No. It's his general attitude," Annis said, scowling. "He shows no interest in Chantley. He never attends village functions. never contributes anything towards fairs and things. He's mean, considering his vast wealth. . . Oh, I almost forgot. He gave two free passes to his North Wales leisure park as a draw prize at the village fete last summer! Huh, big deal!

"Maybe he doesn't realize he should support things," Nicky suggested.

"Oh come off it!" Annis threw a sideways look. "Old Mr Parks-Harrison always attended the Summer Fete. He used to judge the produce and Mrs P-H provided strawberry teas. They donated a silver trophy for the best kept cottage. They mingled, took an interest in their tenants. Gregory never shows his face from one year to the next!"

"That's because he's got a business to run. He's always mad busy. Your Mr P-H only had Chantley to occupy him. There's a difference."

Annis gave a snort of disgust. "You can say that again!"

Nicky was silent. From what her father had said of Nigel Gregory he seemed a tolerant, approachable character, popular in his own circle and certainly respected. Seeing him just now with Pru supported this. Besides, their outing could be quite innocent.

"Perhaps he was giving Pru a lift somewhere," she suggested in an attempt to smooth things. "At the last rally she was going on about how her car was playing up, remember?"

"There are spare vehicles at the Manor!" Annis snapped. "Mrs P-H's, or there's Dobs always at beck and call. Whose side are you on anyway?"

"Why, Chantley's of course!" Nicky was stung by Annis's tone. "But it IS difficult with Dad working for Gregory. I wish he didn't, then I'd be free to hate the man as soundly as everyone else."

Annis looked daggers. "I don't see what that's got to do with it. You're either for this leisure scheme and the destruction of the meadows or you're not!"

"You know the answer to that," Nicky said, her voice bruised and quiet. She drew a quivering breath. "Maybe once we've seen Felix and get more information, we'll see things in a clearer light."

Annis did not reply, having lapsed into sulks, and they had reached the pillared entrance to Chantley House before she spoke again.

"Not up the drive", she said, hastily. "Gregory may return and spot us. If we cut through the meadows we can sneak in the back way. There's a games room over the garages. Pool table, darts, computer games and such. All very swish. Likely we'll find Felix there, he's an early riser."

"Goodness!" Nicky exclaimed, reining in Cobber to let Annis take the lead. "How do you know all this?"

Good humour restored, Annis dimpled. "Well Bob Merridew, who's Gregory's handyman-cum-gardener told his dad, who told his brother, who mentioned it to Dobs. Apparently they're drinking partners. And Dobs was down the forge last week, getting the hunters shod for cubbing."

"Some grapevine!" said Nicky. Squinting over the garden wall at the house, she wondered afresh at the empty stables, the deserted paddocks. Mentioning this,

Annis was cutting.

"Most likely because it's the thing to have! You build yourself a country house, then you get the trimmings. Like horses. And huge rampaging dogs which are allowed to run amok amongst the sheep—"

"I didn't know Gregory had a dog," said Nicky.

Annis only looked sour. "He hasn't, but give him time!"

They walked the ponies single file along the narrow path. Birds twittered cheerfully. From somewhere a cow moaned a reminder that it was milking time. A fresh little breeze teased the grasses, and on it hung the mingled scents of gorse and heather from the distant heath. Miraculously recovered from the recent drought, the meadows were green and flower-spangled. If Nigel Gregory's development scheme succeeded, all this would be destroyed. Nicky felt a shiver touch her.

They were nearing the rear of the house, which gave off on to paddocks, when Tiffin launched into one of his long huffles. Annis gave his neck a reassuring pat. But then Cobber flung up his head and whickered. Annis reined in abruptly. "It's Zak Shone," she hissed over her shoulder. "Talking to Felix!"

"But Zak swore he didn't know Felix," said Nicky, craning to look.

"Oh, you never can trust Zak," Annis muttered. "His dad was the same, always lying through his teeth! I bet he taught Zak a few things, like disguising horses by dyeing their coats and doping them with herbal drugs. AND driving nails between their shoes to stave off a lame look."

Nicky was aghast. She was familiar with the dyeing,

but the rest?

"—Not to mention rasping teeth!" Annis nodded. "There was no end to his tricks."

"Rasping teeth? But why?"

Annis tutted. "You ARE an innocent! To make a horse appear younger of course! They burn into the core of the tooth as well. My dad says a clever gypsy can take ten years off a horse's age, no problem!" She glanced ahead. "Come on, Felix is waving. What d'you bet Zak's selling him a pony and he wants our opinion?"

Nicky followed helplessly. Her mind was spinning, and her gaze was fixed on the paddock gate, to which a bright bay gelding with a neat head and immaculately pulled mane and tail was secured. His outline was terribly, IMPOSSIBLY familiar! So was the way he pawed the ground.

Noticing them, the bay flung up his head and gave a shrill whinny.

That confirmed it. Nicky's fingers went nerveless on the reins. Reaching the boys, they slid to the ground. Zak's scowl told Nicky that he was far from pleased at the intrusion.

Annis greeted Zak coolly but turned a beaming smile on Felix. "Hi! We were passing and thought we'd drop by."

"Great." A responding grin broke over Felix's pleasant, sun-tanned face. He gestured towards the pony, which still sidled restlessly on its tether. "Zak here's brought that little bay for me to try out. What d'you make of it?"

Felix spoke with an easy American drawl and when he smiled his eyes creased up, as if they were smiling too. He was the sort of person you instantly warmed to, Nicky decided. Annis was obviously of the same mind, the way she was dimpling and flapping her eyelashes. Evidently her dislike of Nigel Gregory did not extend to his son.

Tilting her head to one side, Annis studied the bay. "He seems agitated," she said dubiously. "Is he a youngster?"

"Guess so," Felix said. "Zak says he's got jumping potential but needs bringing on. He's just what I had in mind. Pop's offered to find something on loan, but I prefer to buy even though it'll only be for a few weeks, and that's OK by Pop."

Annis eyed Felix doubtfully. He was even taller than Roger. "That bay's small for you," she ventured, ignoring Zak's daggered look. "A 13.2 might be better."

Felix shook his head. "Size doesn't worry me. I'll have to sell him on before I go back home, anyway. I just want something to ride while I'm over here, but not a MADE pony. I like a challenge!" He laughed, a bit self-consciously.

Zak's eyes darted from one to the other, following the conversation carefully. "I reckon that little 'oss fills the bill then, don't he?" he urged. "You won't get none more genuine than Zephyr!"

Nicky stared accusingly. "What did you call him?"

"Zephyr," Zak repeated in all innocence. He gave his polished boots a casual flip with his whip. "Want to try him?"

"No, I don't," Nicky returned coldly. Zak's face split into a grin.

Annis cleared her throat. "Er, I wouldn't mind a try," she said. "I've never ridden a young pony before."

"Fine!" exclaimed Felix. "I'll go shorten up the stirrups. Come when you're ready. . ." Smiling benignly, he wandered off to the pony. Zak shrugged and followed.

Shakily Annis handed Tiffin's rein to Nicky. "Oh heck, you never know what to expect with Zak's stock," she muttered, as if she were having second thoughts. "Oh well, here goes."

Nicky swallowed. "Don't," she pleaded. "Let's go. We can always come back another time. I don't like the look of that pony." She clutched the two sets of reins worriedly and sent the bay a troubled glance.

"YOU GETTIN' ON THIS 'OSS TODAY OR TOMORRA?" yelled Zak. He had untied the pony and was standing by its head. Felix was adjusting the stirrups.

Annis drew a seething breath. "Zak Shone's a pain!" she hissed, squaring her shoulders. "I bet he thinks I can't manage his beastly nag, but I'm jolly well going to show him!"

She stalked off. Heart in her mouth, Nicky watched Felix leg her up. Indignation must have lent Annis courage, because she looked extremely confident as she gathered the reins and clicked her tongue. The bay sprang forward with quick, short strides. Annis urged him away from the group and out into the emerald expanse of meadow.

Nicky recalled Comet's love of wide open spaces, the way his tail gave that warning flick, the determined toss of the head and the wild, uncontrollable gallop that followed. She hardly dared watch and her hands were sweaty on the ponies' reins.

To be fair, the bay went superbly. Annis circled him at a walk and trot and pushed him into a canter. He sprang willingly on the correct leg. No sign of jibbing, no hint of a buck, no bombing off. His brownish ears were tight-pricked, his intelligent eyes shone. Nicky was puzzled. Perhaps this was not Comet after all.

Zak sniffed impatiently. "GET HIM MOVIN'!" he hollered, and Nicky saw the pony's ears come back to his voice in a swift, Comet-like fashion. "LET HIM GO!"

Don't, Nicky begged silently. But Annis had already gathered the reins. The bay took off like a racehorse. Annis leaned forward in the saddle, her face glowing, her long golden hair fanning out behind her. Neck outstretched, tail pluming, Zephyr skimmed over the flat meadowland with hooves that barely seemed to touch the grass.

Nicky felt her throat constrict. They would make a fabulous picture. She also had to suppress a small, unworthy twinge of jealously. SHE could never have found the courage to mount the bay and gallop him like that. But then Annis was unaware of the pony's background, she consoled herself.

Zak was regarding her with that infuriating smirk that said all. "Zephyr goes a treat, don't he?" he taunted.

Nicky tightened her lips. Annis was bringing the pony back to them at a bouncing canter. She halted him smoothly. "He really is FUN!" she cried. "So eager and FAST! I wouldn't mind him myself!"

"You look fine on him!" said Felix. "I guess he IS more your size than mine."

At this Zak's face darkened. Nicky affected indifference. Annis, blissfully ignorant of any undertones, gave Zephyr's neck a hearty slap.

"Care to jump him?" prompted Felix. "Pop's had a makeshift manege built round the back. C.mon!" And without waiting for a reply he grabbed the bay's head and led him off.

Nicky waited till they were out of earshot, and then she rounded on Zak furiously. "That's Comet, isn't it? You've stained him brown but I'd know him anywhere! Zak, how COULD you?"

Zak merely sniggered. "What's bugging you? That 'oss is a little bay I broke meself."

"Oh, come off it!" Nicky exclaimed. "It IS Comet, isn't it?" Zak just stood, grinning his infuriating grin. "PLEASE don't sell him to Felix," Nicky continued in growing panic. "He's sure to ride him to the rallies and Mum'll see. Mum's no fool. She'll RECOGNIZE Comet by his jumping. He flicks his hind hooves and jerks his nose."

"Snatches," Zak put her right. "He don't do that now—or he'd best not, after all my work!"

"Then it IS Comet?" Nicky cried triumphantly.

Zak glowered. "I nivver said that, did I? Buys in a lot of 'osses, don't I? Zephyr could be any one of 'em."

"I've a bone to pick with you over Cobber as well," Nicky snapped. "He's old, isn't he? That's why he gets out of breath during games. You burned his teeth to make him look younger."

Zak's lip curled. "Who told you that fairytale?"

"I just know," said Nicky. "I'm not STUPID!"

"You could o' fooled me!" Zak said with a sneer.

Drawing a long breath, Nicky tried again, persuasively this time. "Zak, you can't do this. It's not on, dyeing horses to make them look different. What happens when they lose their coats and turn back to their original colour? Don't the owners come gunning for you?"

"Don't be daft," Zak muttered. "I ain't such a fool as to sell 'em local, am I?"

"Zephyr's local enough!" replied Nicky. "I wouldn't mind betting he'll be competing at Chantley Show."

"Nick," Zak shook his head reprovingly. "You got to trust me!"

"Trust YOU?" Nicky cried, fear and frustration kicking up inside her. "I'd sooner trust the DC! Or. . . or. . ." She cast about wildly. "Or Nigel Gregory! Annis warned me about you, Zak Shone. She said you hoodwinked people and she was right!"

Zak's face went suddenly grim. Fists clenched, he launched himself forward with a savage sureness. Nicky stood her ground, gripping the ponies' reins till her knuckles whitened, and braced herself for the blow.

Reaching her, Zak pulled to a heaving halt. His nostrils were flared, his features twisted with rage. Nicky could smell the stink of the stable that was strong about him, and she saw him for what he was—a no-good tinker with vengeance on his mind.

Passing a hand across his forehead Zak made as if to speak, but instead the swung on his heels and stalked away, the lines of his shoulders and set of his dark head rigid with pent-up anger.

Cobber watched him go and gave a soft little whicker. Nicky pulled his head round peevishly. She found herself cold and trembling. Her hand flew to her eyes, where a telltale thrumming had begun.

Minutes later there was a thunder of hooves and the bay went streaking away over the meadows, hell-bent for the forest, with Zak spurring him on like a jockey nearing the finishing post.

"What's bugging him?" Annis cried, approaching from the paddock area alone.

"Haven't a clue," Nicky said. "He just went. Where's Felix?"

"Gone to ring his old man. He's keen to have Zephyr. Huh, it must be great to be able to fork out like that, money no object."

Nicky swallowed hard. "Did you find out Zak's price? Not that the bay's worth much. He's just another misfit!"

Annis looked at her strangely. "I thought you and Zak were buddies.

"Oh really? I can't think what gave you that idea!"

Annis shrugged, then said breathlessly, "You'll never believe it. Felix says Zak wants in the region of a THOUSAND POUNDS for that bay because of his jumping potential. Phenomenal, isn't it? Knowing Zak, he'll get it. And oh, Nicky, you should have come to watch. It's some manege, considering it's supposed to be makeshift! The jumps are fantastic!" Annis gave a little gasping laugh.

Unmoved, Nicky handed over Tiffin's reins and climbed wearily on to Cobber. Her head was throbbing fiercely now, the first migraine since that day—it seemed an age ago—when she had met Zak and sampled Marcia's headache remedy.

Annis vaulted lightly up on Tiffin, something she could now do with ease. "Let's go home by Home Farm," she said. "We're less likely to meet up with Gregory that way!" They rode the ponies out of the meadow and on to the road.

The morning was warming up. The first heady chorus

of birdsong was over and a great golden sun was rising over the frilled line of the forest. People were up and about. A milk tanker chugged carefully past, the driver smiling and waving his hand to the two riders. There was the rumble of a tractor. Distantly, a combine harvester was threshing in what it could of the storm-wrecked corn.

They came to Home Farm, where a cockerel flapped to the top of a steaming midden and crowed for all he was worth. A dog barked on the end of its chain and a flurry of little piglets ran squealing from their stone sty. There was a pungent ripeness to the air.

The girls had to rein in sharply as the yardgate swung open and a huge herd of Friesians began to spill out. Nicky watched their lumbering progress across the lane and sighed, giving Cobber's solid chestnut neck a pat. A few gingery hairs came away on her palm. Looking closer, there seemed a lot of white mingling with the chestnut.

Alarm shivered through her. Now that she had rowed with Zak, her Big Secret weighed heavier than ever on her conscience.

"We never did pump Felix over the leisure park," Annis said.

Nicky shook her aching head and tried to marshal her thoughts. There was something about this enmity between the village and Nigel Gregory that niggled her. "Annis, how long ago was Chantley sold?"

"Oh. . ." Annis's brow wrinkled. "Before the Tinies. Around five years I guess. Why?"

"Just curious. Did Zak's father work for Gregory at all?"

"Sort of. I only know what Dad's said. Apparently Gregory's house took AGES to build. By the time he came to move in the place had become very run down. Zak's dad just sort of. . . lost heart. Didn't rear any game or clear the trails or do any of the things keepers are supposed to do. When Gregory saw how neglected the forest and land had become there was a blazing row, with Mrs P-H in the middle. Instead of Mrs P-H siding with Zak's dad, as he'd expected, she accused him of idling. My Dad says it was a case of everyone blaming each other, when really they were all responsible for the upkeep of the place."

Nicky could imagine the DC, bitter at having lost her precious land and properties. And Zak's father, set in his ways, viewing the enforced change in his lifestyle with hatred and distrust. Gregory would have come eagerly to Chantley, expecting the well-run and trim estate he had bought and finding instead rampant chaos.

"Anyway Zak's dad made off. The rest you know," Annis finished.

"So Nigel Gregory hasn't always been uninterested in the estate. He was concerned about it initially?" Nicky probed.

"I suppose so."

"Didn't he get another keeper?"

"He tried, but no one wanted the job."

Nicky's look was hard. "You mean no one would consider working for the new owner—for Gregory? People were suspicious of change and they reacted by refusing to cooperate, and Gregory blew his top?"

Annis shifted uneasily in the saddle. "Something like that?"

"Then I guess Chantley's as much to blame as Nigel Gregory for the rift," Nicky said shortly.

Annis did not answer. The last cow trailed across with a huff of milky breath. The cowman slammed the gate and, with a cheery nod to the girls, went indoors for his breakfast.

TWELVE

It was at the next rally, the last before Chantley Show, that Nicky spotted the solitaire diamond ring on Pru's finger.

Nicky did her best to catch Annis's eye as they circled for a warm-up game of musical sacks and consequently missed the pause. So when Cobber did his shoot to the centre they parted company, with Nicky ending up sprawled on the ground. This prompted a sharp reprimand from Pru.

"Oh wake up, Nicky! Comet was doing fine but you were daydreaming! We'll never get a team together at this rate!"

"Sorry!" Nicky mumbled, pulling herself to her feet. Annis darted a sympathetic look. Roger grinned wryly, the twins laughed outright. Lisa looked down her nose and Mo thoughtfully ruffled Dinah Mite's mane. Nicky knew how badly the girl coveted a mount such as Cobber. She also realized that Mo would not have allowed herself to be distracted, no way.

Red-faced, Nicky caught Cobber and remounted.

Nearby Mrs Flynn was giving enthusiastic encouragement to her Smalls on Shetlands. She had them well organized now, with a mother to each pony and every child more or less aware of what each game entailed. Mrs Davis, as usual, was haring from group to group with notebook in hand. The DC's voice carried stridently from the manege, where she was instructing showjumping. Dobs' more tolerant tones drifted from the working hunter group.

Pru flicked 'A Hunting We Will Go' to full volume and Nicky winced. A week of broken nights, in which her mind wrestled with ponies, leisure parks and empty schoolrooms, had left her sleepy-eyed and edgy.

Cobber's pace was smooth, the rhythmic plod of hooves soporific, and it was not long before the music seemed to go far away and Nicky's eyelids began to droop. But then the band stopped, and when Cobber made his dash for the centre Nicky again found herself biting the dust.

"DISQUALIFIED!" yelled Pru furiously.

Smarting under her reproachful glare, Nicky made another muttered apology, grabbed Cobber and led him off. Cobber lowered his head to doze and Nicky leaned back against the paddock rails reflectively.

The day was calm, and everything lay gently green and contented under the whitish August skies. A couple of full-bellied brood mares grazed the nearby pasture, but the 'chasers were in, a long line of noble heads peering inquisitively over their half-doors on to the Manor's paved yard. Nicky's fingers had itched to draw them.

Some day, she planned, she would pluck up courage and ask the DC's permission to come and sketch freely. It was sad that only half the stables were in use, but on paper she could depict the yard as it used to be when Mr Parks-Harrison owned Chantley, and that shuttered row of loose-boxes rang to the clop of restless hooves and the cheerful whistling of stable lads.

Annis was next to be thrown out, Tiffin being more interested in Dinah Mite than his rider's aids.

"THE REST OF YOU KEEP ALERT!" Pru jabbed the on-switch impatiently and the ponies circled.

"She gets more like her ma every day," grumbled Annis, who still had not forgiven Pru for siding with the enemy. Slipping down, she loosened Tiffin's girth and turned a gloomy face on Nicky. "Did you spot that ring?"

"Could I miss it?" Nicky countered. "I was dazzled!"

"I reckon they were on they way to Ludlow to buy it the day they almost mowed us down," Annis said. "I told you Pru was all-a-bundle. And thinking about it, she's not daft. See what she stands to gain." Her look embraced fields, forest and the distant village.

"Chantley?" Nicky was thoughtful. "The family estate restored? Maybe you're right."

"You bet I am! And much good will it do her when the place is turned into a playground!" Annis said acidly. "There'll be no room for 'chasers then. No hunting either. "Pru'll find herself managing a stream of tourists instead of ponies!"

"DON'T FORGET TO KEEP UP YOU IMPULSION! GET YOUR HORSE ON THE BIT!" cut in Mrs Parks-Harrison's voice enthusiastically. The show-jumpers were now limbering up with a spot of preliminary dressage and the two girls glanced across. Nicky's eyes flicked anxiously from one intent, dark-capped rider to the next. No sign of Felix and Zephyr. Maybe he'd had second thoughts over the pony's size and decided against buying it after all. Nicky's spirits lifted slightly.

"If you're looking for Felix, he's with Dobs and the working hunters," Annis declared shrewdly. "Someone must have loaned him a mount after all, because he's not on Zak's bay."

Nicky strained to see and sure enough, jumping a classy-looking steel grey over a set of natural obstacles was Felix Gregory. So he hadn't bought Zephyr! Nicky let out a breath of pure relief.

Annis was regarding her curiously. "You didn't like Zak's bay, did you? she said.

Nicky affected a shrug. "I neither liked nor disliked it," she said, avoiding Annis' gaze. "It was just another pony."

She began to fiddle unhappily with the buckle on Cobber's rein. Everything was going sour. Since their quarrel Zak had not showed up for an early morning ride, which was hardly surprising. She had visited Keeper's Lodge several times but Zak had been absent. Schooling a new 'oss in the forest, Marcia had said. Nicky knew that he was avoiding her and had convinced herself that she did not really mind. But on its heel had come regret. Really she wanted to make things right with Zak. She just did not know how to go about it.

Last evening Marcia had been up to the elbows in cotton sheeting, which she had dyed to rainbow hues and was snipping into buntings for the gymkhana. Nicky offered help with the sewing, but her skill with a pencil did not stretch to needlework, and grimacing at her cobbled stitches, Marcia sent her out to water and feed the animals.

She wandered morosely from pen to pen. The sow badger had gone but the barn owl was still there. Although his wing was mended, he lacked the strong flight feathers needed before he could be set free. He had never taken to captivity and huddled in his cage, watching Nicky mournfully with his round black eyes which said over and over again: 'trapped, trapped.'

Nicky knew precisely how he felt.

"COME ON, YOU TWO PRIZE MISERIES! INTO LINE!"

Nicky surfaced to find Pru waving them over. "And this time, Annis Reed and Nicky McGuire, KEEP ALERT!"

Mounting swiftly, the girls went to join the team. The music sounded and Cobber fell enthusiastically into step behind Tiffin, whom Annis had been careful to place away from Dinah Mite. Nicky fixed her gaze on Cobber's ears and when, the second the music stopped, they gave a tiny flick, she was ready. Leaping down, she ran with him to the centre and neatly claimed her sack.

"Better!" Pru said, with a warning, "and don't you ever let that brilliant chestnut down again!"

After the dubious start things picked up. Pru ran through each of the games and ended amid many groans with her favourite Walk, Trot and Gallop. The pace was hot. Pru, who never blamed a pony, was also quick to praise the riders where it was due.

"You're learning to stop!" she challenged Tom, when he pulled Snippet to a triumphant halt after the mad scramble to the finishing line. "I'm impressed!"

And, "Jolly good, Daniel!" when he did what Pru had been drumming in all summer, and paid attention. Daniel grinned wickedly and said his brain was awake for once, which was more than he could say for some. Nicky was shot a sideways look.

As this was their final practice everyone—apart from Nicky who found it impossible to shake off her problems—was aware of Pru's critical eye. Sure enough, before lunch break, she called the group together.

"I'm going to give my blunt opinion, of riders and ponies," she informed them, chuckling at their guarded expressions. Her main worry with Dutchman, she told Roger, was his clumsiness. The piebald's height scarcely mattered most times, as Roger was tall and could vault up easily. It was when they rode pairs the problems began, with shortish girls like Mo needing to make massive springs onto the pony's broad back.

"On the plus side, Dutchman is totally unflappable—a big asset in mounted games. You also control him well. I can tell you've put in a great deal of work. Well done!"

Roger's ears went slightly pink but he smiled and gave Dutchman's black and white neck a pat.

Pru's gaze fell on Moonspinner and she sighed. "He's a flighty so-and-so, isn't he!" she said kindly to Lisa, who was trembling on the brink of tears. "Have you cut his oats?"

Lisa flushed crimson. "Um, I. . .I think so. Actually I"m not sure—"

All sympathy fled from Pru's face. "You don't mean to say you still leave his feeding to your mother?" she cried.

Lisa gave a guilty nod. "I'm s. . .sorry. It's just that

Mummy's up at dawn with the hunters. She's done the feeds before I get to the stables and Moonspinner gets the same as the rest."

"That's no excuse!" Pru was livid. "You should get yourself up earlier! Be determined, take an interest in your pony! Oh, honestly, I may as well save my breath!"

Waving a dismissive hand, she went on to the Flynn twins. Their steady cheerfulness was infectious and she found herself smiling. "Well, you two tearabouts! What you lack in skill you certainly make up for in cheek!"

The boys grinned.

"Those Exmoors have loads of potential, you know. Correct size, keen, quick. They'll make perfect gymkhana ponies if you trouble to school them. But I am pleased. Today has shown much improvement. Well done!"

The grins broadened and Pru laughed. Nicky awaited her turn with dread. When it came, her worst fears were realized. "Comet's a terrific pony, I'm just concerned about his breathing when the pace quickens. You might get your vet to look him over. Oh, I don't think for a moment there's anything seriously wrong. . ." Nicky had paled, and Pru smiled encouragingly. "Maybe it was just the heat, getting to him. Your riding is heaps better, Nicky. If you could keep your mind on the job it would improve further."

Pru glanced oh-so-briefly at Mo, and Nicky was beset by the feeling that if she made up a team, Pru might ask Mo to ride Cobber instead of herself. She knew that in mounted games it was a case of the best riders for the keenest ponies.

Pru gave Tiffin's dappled neck a slap. Annis had a good

mount in Tiffin, he just lacked experienced but hopefully that would come. About Mo and her Shetland Pru had nothing but praise.

"It's unfortunate the pony's legs aren't a couple of inches longer. You're always going to find this a handicap." Her smile was regretful. Mo nodded philosophically, and on that thoughtful note Pru dismissed them for lunch.

Annis and Nicky were heading eagerly for the parked trailers and horse-boxes when Nicky's mother, deep in committee talk with the DC and Mrs Scott, suddenly sprang to uncouple the trailer. The three of them then leaped into the car, which roared off across the field and vanished in a cloud of exhaust smoke down the drive.

"There goes my lunch," Nicky wailed. "And I'm absolutely starving!"

"You can join us," Annis offered. "You know Mum always packs enough to feed an army."

They were greeted ecstatically by the Tinies, who danced around the ponies demanding rides.

"Me first!"

"No, I want to be first!"

"You were first last time. Mummy, wasn't Andrea first last time? It's not fair—"

"Lunch!" announced Mrs Reed firmly. "Annabel, fetch the coke. Angie, the cups. Andrea the box of sandwiches." The three little girls bulldozed into action and soon they were all tucking into cheese rolls and cups of Coke. The ponies had been untacked and bundled into halters. Tiffin, tied to the trailer, pulled contentedly at his haynet.

Nicky left Cobber standing free, his blue lead-rope

trailing. As usual he dropped his head and began to doze. At the first rustle of sandwich wrappings, however, his eyes opened. One ear twitched interestedly, his nostrils quivered. . .

And for the first time since Nicky had acquired him, Cobber broke his training and took a step forward. Nicky made a grab for the lead-rope as his nose plunged determinedly into the picnic hamper. Annis chuckled and the Tinies with laughter, but Mrs Reed was not amused.

"Why not tie him up?" she suggested, mindful of her precious food. Nicky was about to confess to the chestnut's bad habit when Pru, doing the rounds in place of her mother, appeared at their site.

She stood briefly, frowning at the havoc. Then without a word she snatched the lead-rope from Nicky's grasp and marched Cobber to the trailer.

Nicky rammed her cheese roll into her mouth and was on her feet instantly. "Pru. . ." she spluttered. "Cobber doesn't t. . ." The rest was lost in a fit of choking. Annis reached over and thumped her soundly on her back, and through streaming eyes Nicky saw Cobber firmly tied to the Reed's ramshackle trailer.

Pru was saying brightly to Mrs Reed, "Now you can have your meal in peace. Mother asked me to give her apologies for rushing off so rudely but she, Mrs Scott and Mrs McGuire have been called urgently to town. An enquiry from the Education Office concerning the school closure—"

A fearsome grunt from behind them made her spin round. Cobber's face wore a look of stubborn disapproval, his head came up, his shoulders strained. Nicky tore to his side.

It was too late. . . Cobber was already fighting. The trailer swayed alarmingly and Annis leaped, shrieking, to Tiffin's rescue. There were shouts of "whoa there!" and "Mind!" Mrs Reed swooped up the Tinies. Nicky tried to yank free the slip-knot. Pru sprang to help Nicky. Cobber, plunging and heaving in total oblivion of anything but the urge to be free, gave one last violent breenge and the lead-rope was jerked from Nicky"s hands.

"Ouch!" she yelped at the quick, searing pain. Dodging sideways to avoid Mrs Reed and the Tinies, Cobber gave his head a youthful toss and went barging off down the field.

"LOOSE HORSE!" yelled Pru, hurling herself in pursuit.

Her cry was echoed down the line. Mothers, grooms and riders poured from their cars to try and head the pony off, but it was useless. Cobber slipped shadow-like through their ranks and charged on. Past the paddocks, hell-bent for the Manor with Nicky, Pru and Annis puffing red-faced in his wake.

Blood pounding in her ears, Nicky put on a desperate spurt. Skirting the front of the house, crossing the lawn, dodging the fragrant garden. Cobber was now a chestnut speck in the distance.

Skidding to a halt beneath a rose-smothered pergola, Nicky saw his tail disappear with a flourish beneath the arched entrance to the stable yard. There was a clatter of hooves on the paved ground, followed by several startled whinnies.

Nicky felt a cool shower of pink petals on her bare

arm and Annis came to a heaving stop beside her. "Whatever's bugged Comet?" she gasped crossly. "He's normally so sensible!"

Nicky did not answer. Her gaze was on Pru, who had come up on her other side and whose perspiring face was taking on a look of stunned disbelief.

"I wonder if. . .? But no, it CAN'T be! And yet he used to do. . ." Pru darted forward, covering the ground with a few rapid bounds. Nicky followed woodenly with Annis mystified beside her.

Cobber had come to a blowing halt by an end stall, which was occupied by a tall bay thoroughbred. His velvet, aristocratic nose investigated the sweaty pony curiously. Long, pointed ears went back and he gave a playful squeal, striking a forehoof on the floor with a sound like a pistol shot. The door of the groom's flat opened smartly and Dob's head appeared.

"Now then, now then, what's going on?" he called. he stepped out, chipped mug in one hand and sandwich in the other. When he saw Cobber, he came to an astonished halt. "Why, it if ain't young Nicky McWhatsit's little chestnut!"

All set to bluff it out, Nicky darted up and took the broken halter. "C. . .Comet's been really bad! I don't know what came over him, perhaps a fly stung. . ."

Her voice trailed. Pru was running a trembling hand along the pony's steaming neck. Removing it, she frowned at her damp palm, which now sported a liberal coating of chestnut hair. She walked around him, smoothing his mane, sliding her fingers familiarly along his sturdy back and down his sloping quarters. She flicked his tail, felt his legs, glanced into his mouth. . .and made a sour face.

Lastly she looked into his eyes, and her own became suddenly moist. Straightening, she met Dobs' puzzled gaze and said chokingly but with utmost certainty, "Dobs, what do you bet that despite the youthful teeth and trimmed mane and tail, that under this disgusting chestnut stain is my dear old Dandy?"

THIRTEEN

"I could SUE that dealer's yard," fumed Nicky's mother as she watched the gymkhana finalists gather into the collecting ring. "It's made me look so incompetent, buying a chestnut that turns out a mere skewbald!"

"Oh honestly, Mum!" Nicky tightened Cobber's girth, pulled down the stirrups and mounted briskly. "I don't care what colour Comet is. He's a brilliant gymkhana pony and that's all that matters."

Nicky's face glowed. Cobber had qualified for all four finals and nothing, not even her mother's grievances, could take away the glorious satisfaction of the moment. Mum, thrilled at Nicky's success but still nursing a bruised ego, gave a tight smile.

Chantley Horse Show and Gymkhana was held by tradition on the meadows. The sun shone warmly and the McGuires were seated on blue folding chairs by the ringside. At their feet, an open picnic basket displayed cans of beer and Mum's favourite low calorie fruit drinks.

Mum's gaze skimmed over the mixed bunch of ponies,

paused briefly on Tiffin whom Annis had turned out splendidly, and came to rest with longing on Lisa's glossy-coated and elegant Moonspinner. "Now THAT'S what I call a decent mount," she approved. "A pony to be proud of."

Her voice had an edge to it and Dad, who was indulging in a rare day off and wanted nothing more than to sit in the sun and watch the events, said, "Nicky's proud enough of—er—Comet, aren't you Nick?" Nicky gave a wearied nod. "So let's not worry, eh?"

Mum turned on him reproachfully. "Comet, or Dandy or whatever his name is, was tennish when Pru lost him. That was five years ago. How long do you think Nicky's going to be able to tear about on him doing gymkhana games?"

Dad looked bemused. "I haven't a clue. But I thought Pru had him vetted?"

"She did," Nicky cut in, giving Cobber's neck a supportive pat. "He's perfectly sound and good for ages yet."

"But I paid the earth for a thoroughbred!"Mum argued bitterly. "The dealer said—"

"Never mind all that," said Dad soothingly. "Comet's a grand fellow. Nicky dotes on him and Pru's delighted that he's found and is in good hands."

Mum though, was not to be pacified. "We've been hoodwinked," she muttered. "Dobs swears that staining was a gypsy job."

Nicky kept her lips tight closed. Throughout all the tedius anguishing of the past days she had uttered not one word which might implicate the Shones, and she intended to keep it that way.

Dad, who considered the whole situation one huge

joke, was now chuckling. "You've got to hand it to them, those gypsies sure know their stuff! That chestnut stain had everyone fooled, including Pru and Mrs P-H!"

"It is NOT funny!" Mum sounded furious and Dad was swift to arrange his face into more sympathetic lines.

A shout from the collecting ring brought Nicky's head up. "That's Pru," she said, hastily gathering her reins. "Oh heck, come on boy!" She rode away, her parents' good luck wishes loud in her ears.

Mum drew a long breath. Dad reached for a beer and sank back in his chair, smiling at her placatingly. "Relax. Think of your other news, eh?"

The morning post had brought a letter, bearing an official stamp and addressed to The Chantley Save Our School Committee. It had stated briefly that due to increased public pressure, and following their discussion on the 24th August—which had been the day of the last rally, when committee members had been swiftly summoned to County Hall for interview—the hitherto plans for the closure of Chantley Primary School were temporarily shelved.

Mum had read the words over twice before dashing triumphantly to the telephone. Feverishly she had poured her news into Mrs Parks-Harrisons's unbelieving ear. "But we mustn't become too complacent," she finished on a warning note. "That's what these people wait for. They look for a crack in the resolve, then they pounce! We must carry on fighting."

Despite this reservation the glad news travelled fast. Over breakfast, Chantley celebrated its victory. The organizers were jubilant when they met up at the showground.

"Round one to us!" Mrs Parks-Harrison boomed to Mrs Davies.

"Indeed yes," Mrs Davies agreed. Smiling broadly, she watched the DC stomp off to welcome the Working Hunter Judge.

The PTA members, who had done much to back Karen McGuire's ranks, strolled about wearing extremely smug expressions. Mrs Scott's frosty face held a glint of satisfaction as she stepped from her Range Rover and went to help Lisa unload Moonspinner. Mrs Flynn had halted the horsebox outside the village pub and purchased a flagon of cider. The twins refused to believe her when she insisted that it was to toast their success, and teased her mercilessly the whole way to the show.

"All due to that Mrs McWhatsit and her letters going hither and thither," Dobs declared to Mr Reed, who was attending the show in the official capacity of farrier. Dobs never would forget the day he was sent out by Mrs P-H to post a letter in one of the freakiest thunderstorms in living memory. Each time he told the tale it became vastly embroidered; the thunder more booming, the lightning fiercer, the drifting hail more hazardous.

The gymkhana ringside was filling up now, the spectators settling themselves with ice creams and cooling soft drinks. Everywhere was bustle and noise. A band played cheerfully, and people not watching the events either chatted in groups or wandered around the stalls. Marcia's handiwork was much in evidence, with banners abundantly displayed, and young and old wearing jazzy tee-shirts bearing the current logo—everything and anything to further the campaign!

In-hand showing was just finishing in the main ring to scattered applause. To one side, a Working Hunter course was set out with wildly-spaced natural obstacles. In the showjumping ring the jumps were varied, brightly painted and craftily placed to test the skills of rider and horse. Nicky's mother eyed them wistfully.

An inventive Handy Pony course, laid out in a far corner, was presided over by Mrs Scott and her assistant, Mrs Stephens. Mo's mother confessed that Handy Pony was her only experience of competition so far, it being their Dinah Mite's forte.

Mrs Flynn was in charge of clear-round jumping. This was not due to open until ten, when the Smalls' mounted games—also Mrs Flynn's province—would hopefully be over.

There were three gymkhana classes: class One for eight years and under, which was leading rein; class Two for twelve years and under, and class Three, which was for thirteen years and over. All classes had the same four races; Bending, Flag, Apple in the Bucket and Sack. There were rosettes up to four places in each final, to be presented at the conclusion of the games.

Class One came to a riotous finish and Mrs Flynn tore off to her clear-round course where a queue was already gathered. Pru, in sunshine-yellow jeans and toning shirt, dashed furiously up and down organizing the Flag course, whilst Dobs checked the bending poles; one or two of which leaned precariously after the chance encounters with barging Shetlands. Dobs, who had hoped gymkhana events to be a thing of the past, directed many longing glances towards his favoured Working Hunter ring.

All Chantley members had qualified for the finals, if only by the skin of their teeth which was the case with Mo and Lisa—Mo because other ponies were vastly swifter than Dinah Mite, and Lisa because she failed to manage Moonspinner.

Nicky hugged her victory to herself. Cobber was the only pony in the group to qualify in all four sections. The twins had only got into two.

"I'm in Bending and Apple," announced Tom.

"That means I'm up against you in the Apple," grumbled his twin. "But at least I'm in the Sack." Daniel had grinned when he had seen there was a sack race, as it was his best. Roger and Dutchman were in the Bending, Flag and Sack. Annis had also qualified for three; the Bending, Apple and Sack.

"Don't forget we've still each to get a first or second in the finals, or there'll be no PPP!" Roger warned, noting the hordes of gymkhana enthusiasts, most of them chucked out during the heats but hanging on to watch.

Lisa's fingers played nervously in Moonspinner's mane. "I've gone all to pieces," she whinged. "I've only got one chance in the Flag and Moonspinner's being so naughty." The black, as usual, was refusing to stand, causing a despairing Lisa to walk him in endless circles.

Mo glanced up from Dinah Mite's lowly saddle with a sigh. "Given a good mount, I wouldn't know the meaning of nerves," she declared, not boastfully but with quiet conviction. "Dinah's a gem and Mum and Dad can't afford another so I'll have to make do. But I would LOVE something decent to ride."

"Like a chestnut that turns skewbald?" said Daniel, laughing. Amused faces turned on Nicky.

"Mum still hasn't got over the shock," she groaned. "And it took AGES to get that chestnut stain off."

Unlike her mother Nicky was pleased with the results. Cobber gleamed from the tip of his splodgy nose to his flowing, multi-coloured tail. His chestnut patches shone against the white, which was impressively free from grass and stable stains. Nicky had oiled his hooves. Not being accomplished at plaiting, she had left his mane free. it stood bushily along his crested neck, the wisping forelock giving him an endearingly quizzical expression.

Across the ring sat Mrs Reed with the Tinies. Each child wore faded jeans and sloppy, 'save-our-school' tee-shirts. Spying Annis and Nicky, they waved their plump little starfish hands and squealed a greeting. They were promptly hushed by their mother.

"If they show me up I'll DIE of embarrassment!" Annis muttered to Nicky, who was straining over the heads of the crowds towards the Working Hunter ring. Felix Gregory was there, mounted on the grey he rode to the rally. No sign of Zephyr. Nicky offered a silent prayer of thanks.

"FINALISTS FOR THE BENDING, PLEASE!" announced Pru importantly.

There was a stir as riders tussled with unwilling ponies. Cobber though, moved into place like the true veteran he was. Nicky glanced down the starting line: Annis, Roger, Tom and two strangers to challenge.

Pru stood watchfully. Dobs raised the whistle to his lips. Silence fell. Eyes were narrowed, bodies poised for the one off. Cobber gave a little snort.

The whistle blew and the race was on, with Cobber and Tiffin going all out, their hooves pounding and necks outstretched. Weaving expertly between the poles, the girls leaned this way that, steering with weight and reins. Reaching the top, Nicky cursed when she failed to bring Cobber round tightly and lost valuable seconds. This gave Tiffin a lead. Cobber put on a spurt, but he had lost too much ground and was finally beaten into third place by an outsider boy on a nifty dun. Fourth place went to a bespectacled girl on a dappled grey, but Tiffin had won.

Roger thundered in pulling a rueful face, for Dutchman had left a trail of fallen poles behind him on the homeward run. Tom trundled up on foot as Snippet, much to his mortification, had unshipped him in the middle of the race and was now belting riderless across the showground, a stream of well-intentioned spectators on his heels.

"Better get after the wretch!" grumbled Dobs. Tom ran.

Cobber was sweating. "Poor old boy!" Pru said fondly, pausing to slap his patchy rump. To Annis she cried, "Well done! Super start!"

Mrs Reed was beaming proudly. The Tinies were ecstatic. Nicky met her mother's slightly pensive gaze. There were still three more races to go. She wished there had been a Musical Sacks, which was Cobber's best.

"FLAG RACE FINALISTS!" yelled Pru. Everyone surged across to the track, which was set out at intervals with rows of yellow cones, all awaiting their flags.

Roger was in the line-up, grimly determined. Lisa was here too, her face white and strained beneath her smart black hat.

The whistle shrilled. Nicky grabbed her first flag and

let Cobber go. The skewbald went his fastest and was even ahead at the final flag, but on the homeward run he was not match for thundering Dutchman or the outsider boy on the speedy dun. Dutchman won, the dun coming second and Cobber was again third. A boy on a Welsh cross was fourth. Fifth was a small plaited-up bay, whose sulky rider burst into tears when she realized that she was not placed and was promptly pounced upon by a fuming mother and told she had not tried. Moonspinner came in a head-snatching last, with Lisa hauling frantically on her reins.

"Tough luck!" Annis cried.

"Will you leave that poor creature's mouth ALONE!" Pru hissed sideways to Lisa. "Remember what I've taught you!"

"I'm s. . .sorry!" Lisa's face was pale and frightened. "I've gone all to pieces!"

"Oh fiddle!" scoffed Pru, eyeing the black with suspicion. "Your mother's stuffed him with oats for energy, hasn't she!"

When Lisa gave a miserable nod, Pru shook her head hopelessly. Turning to Nicky, her expression became rueful. "Dandy must be feeling his years. In his prime, none of these ponies would have touched him. But don't worry, there's time yet!" Pru laughed her bubbly laugh and chivvied them to the next game which was the Apple in the Bucket, and not Cobber's best because his concentration leaned more to scoffing the apples than racing. Annis was in this. So were the twins. Tom looked cross, as he had only just managed to catch the runaway Snippet. Nicky, horribly aware of her mother's tense face and her father's hopeful stare, waited for the whistle.

Halfway up the track were six blue buckets, each containing four apples to be deposited individually into a corresponding orange bucket, placed at the end of every run. That meant four frantic charges up and down the field under the hot sun—a long pull for Cobber, thought Nicky with a twinge of alarm.

But when the whistle blew the skewbald hurtled off with such enthusiasm that she forgot her fears. She made a concentrated effort to grab the first apple before Cobber could sink his teeth into it. Up to the top at full gallop, racing one-handed and crouched over the pony's neck. A well-aimed fling and the apple was in the bucket before Cobber even saw it. Back to the blue bucket, grab another apple. Charge.

Luscious green fruit came hurtling in all directions and Cobber was practical drooling, but Nicky forced him on, up and down the track at a cracking pace. Hoofbeats pounded, riders cursed, spectators roared. The Tinies shrieked and Nicky's parents sprang to their feet and yelled for her encouragingly. Nicky heard none of it. Hurling the final apple, she wrenched Cobber round and slacking her reins and hollering for all she was worth, raced for the winning post.

"OH JOLLY WELL DONE!" screamed Pru, her face red and beaming. "Good old Dandy! It's the first time he's won the Apple, he always stopped to pig them with me, didn't he, Dobs?"

"That's right," confirmed Dobs. Catching Nicky's eye he added a grudging, "well done!"

"YOU BEAT US HOLLOW!" shrieked Annis, yanking Tiffin to a blowing fourth.

Mum came running up to stuff Cobber with polo

mints and praise Nicky on her terrific riding. Looking round, Nicky now discovered that the second place had gone to a grinning Tom, and third to Daniel.

Daniel was furious. "If you qualify and I don't, I'll never speak to you again," he threatened his other half. There was a short, sharp free-for-all, which was stemmed abruptly by a loud wail from halfway down the track. The boys' heads jerked up.

It was the unsporting girl on the bay.

"Big Sulk!" hissed Tom. "Good thing she's not a candidate for the PPP!!"

They all watched covertly as Big Sulk's mother marched up the field and hauled her daughter off, protesting vociferously to all and sundry that the results were fixed.

"Last race coming up," Pru announced brightly. She turned to the long-suffering Dobs. "Quick, pass me a bucket and shovel please. I'll run up the track and collect left-overs. No one likes falling in a load of you-know-what!"

She tore off, a vivid streak of yellow. To one side, Lisa sat unhappily on a still-fidgeting Moonspinner; she had no chance now of qualifying. Soon Pru was back, giving a thumbs-up to start.

In the line-up was sturdy little Dinah Mite. Mo, clad in her usual well-worn attire, now sported a brand-new skullcap, which she wore proudly without either silk or velvet. Nicky detected Mrs P-H's influence here, for above all else, the Pony Club enforced safety. Headgear in particular.

Dinah Mite's quaint Thelwellian figure, with its glossy mahogany black shine and luxuriant mane and tail, raised many smiles from the ringside, and brought countless oohs and ahs from watching children.

"I want it! I WANT it!" one Tiny was heard to demand. This was promptly enforced by the other two.

Their mother stared at them in sheer perplexity. "But you've seen Dinah Mite often at rallies, and never once have you shown the slightest interest in her!" she protested with her accustomed tolerance.

Three identical pairs of eyes fixed upon their mother imploringly. When patiently told that Dinah Mite was Mo's treasured pet and therefore not for sale, the first Tiny dissolved into tears. "I WANT it!" she wept. "It's not FAIR!"

"It's not FAIR!" the other two echoed.

Nicky urged Cobber next to Mo. Annis nudged in Tiffin. Then came Big Sulk, nervously chewing the top of her whip. Beside her was Daniel on Punch. Finally Roger, thin-lipped and frowning.

Pru eyed the line-up solemnly. Everything depended on this final race. Dobs, now sweating profusely, raised his whistle and blew. The ponies charged, the crowds roared. Nicky's mother was shouting with the rest. The Tinies had stopped bawling and were now screaming for Annis. Roger's mother, who had sneaked away from her Secretary's Tent to watch, stood biting her nails.

Dutchman pounded forward. Reaching the sack, Roger was off and pulling it on. He was a strong, well-made boy, and the vigorous bounds needed to lap the course were nothing to him. He made it easily until, halfway home, his sack bunched and he went sprawling, to be overtaken by Mo and Dinah Mite, and a whooping Daniel with Punch bronco-bucking on the end of his rein.

"GO IT, PUNCH ME LAD!" yelled Daniel, making a final lunge over the winning line.

Mo dragged Dinah Mite into second place. Flinging her arms around the snorting pony's neck, she hugged her soundly and sobbed, "We did it, you beauty, despite your short hairy legs!"

Roger thundered in. Dismounting, he gave a wry grin and made much of Dutchman. Annis, who never had got the hang of running in a sack, was fifth; Big Sulk made a snivelling sixth.

"Not to worry, darling," her mother was heard to pronounce succinctly. "After all it IS Chantley's show"

The seven exchanged disbelieving glances and exploded into ill-disguised chortles. Lisa, who had not exactly felt like laughing, was the first to stop, and one by one, the others too fell silent. They could see Pru at the ringside, conflabbing forcefully with Dobs.

The ultimate moment, when riders would know for certain whether the PPP was on or not, had arrived. Ponies moved restlessly and twitched their tails, riders shifted about in their saddles.

"I. . .I'm most dreadfully sorry," Lisa began to apologize plaintively. "I know I've let everyone down. I'm so sorry!"

"Stop—saying—sorry!" Mo admonished with emphasis. "It isn't your fault if your mother stuffs your pony with oats!"

"But if Pru decides against it it'll be my fault," Lisa wailed, "I really am sorry!"

Her bottom lip trembled. Roger, looking beyond her, gave a shout. "Here's Pru!"

Pru came bounding up, her face wreathed in smiles, her eyes sparkling. "OK, OK, you motley lot!" she cried joyfully. "Guess I'm lumbered! All agreeable to forming a team?"

"Yes!" came the cry in unison. Everyone started talking at once in loud, excited voices. Only Lisa hung back. At once Pru took her to one side.

"You'll have to conquer those nerves," she said, kindly but firmly. "I know Moonspinner's not the easiest ride. Maybe your mother might consider getting another, more suitable mount for you. But till then we're stuck with this one. Let today be a lesson to you. With the correct feeding"—she shot Lisa a hard look—"administered each day by YOU, and not your mother, he WILL improve! Understand?"

Lisa said she did.

"You can come in as reserve," Pru declared on a final note.

Roger yelled three cheers for the Captain. Their voices soared and people stared and Dobs, now gathering in the equipment, smiled resignedly. When the hubbub had died down Pru warned them that if they thought THIS summer's work had been hard, the future was beyond their wildest nightmares. This was accepted with dramatic groans. Tom joked he was thinking of retiring Snippet.

"Don't you dare!" said Pru, grinning.

She then packed them off to the main ring, where, standing behind the presentation table waiting to give out the awards, was none other than Nigel Gregory.

Casual in slacks and open-necked shirt, the business tycoon looked surprisingly at home amongst the gleaming silver trophies and bright-coloured rosettes. Chatting avidly to him, smart in blue linen, was Mrs Parks-Harrison.

Annis' face was a study. "I don't BELIEVE it!" she hissed to Nicky. "After all that trouble between those two!"

Pru went to link her arm in Nigel's and the solitaire ring flashed in the sunlight. Mrs Parks-Harrison gave a brief speech, thanking Nigel Gregory for the loan of his meadow and the competitors for their efforts. She then announced the results of the first race.

Annis gulped and nudged Tiffin forward. She even managed a tight smile as Nigel clipped the red rosette on Tiffin's bridle. The Flag placings were awarded, and then it was Nicky's turn.

Mrs Parks-Harrison's well-defined brows shot up. "Dandy's won the APPLE RACE?" she roared in disbelief. "Good gracious me! He always ate the fruit with Pru!"

"So this is Dandy!" said Nigel Gregory. His mouth twitched.

"Dandy's called Comet now," put in Pru, wrinkling her nose. "It doesn't suit him, not one bit."

Mrs Parks-Harrison patted the pony's neck thoughtfully. "He's had a fresh start with you, Nicolette, so why not rename him?" she suggested with a hint of a smile. "You've done wonders to win the only race that ever defeated Pru!" Her smile broadened. Nicky met her shrewd grey eyes and glimpsed there a certain empathy she had never noticed before.

She had made a spot decision. "Actually, I'm calling him Cobber.

It was the name a friend of mine gave a favourite pony."

Pru and the DC were quick to voice their approval.

"Cobber it is!" Nigel Gregory hooked the red rosette on to the skewbald's bridle and moved on.

Annis pounced on Nicky as she rode from the ring. "What d'you think of him?"

"Well um. . . he was fine."

"You would say that!" Annis snapped. "If you'd lived here when all the trouble was on, you'd think differently. I don't know what's come over the Parks-Harrisons. Surely they could have found someone connected with horses to give the awards."

"Nigel Gregory IS into horses," cut in Tom, eaves-dropping unashamedly, "My dad says he owns a blood-stock stud in Ireland."

"Oh come on!" Annis cried. "MY dad would have known."

Tom gave a careless shrug. "Ask Felix. He's coming over. I'm off. I've a dead mouse I want to put in Ma P-H's drink!"

"You wouldn't DARE!" gasped Nicky.

"Oh wouldn't I?" returned Tom, and digging his heels into Snippet's sides he charged away.

Felix rode up and offered his congratulations. Annis looked pointedly at the green rosette on the grey's bri-dle. "You haven't done so badly yourself."

Felix ran his hand along the grey's crest and said, "Oh, it was all due to Shadow. I just left her to it."

Annis eyed the mare with interest. "She's a nice pony—a better size for you then Zak's bay."

"Sure is!" Felix slapped the grey's neck. "She's not

mine though. She's on loan. I decided not to buy, after all."

Nicky was about to ask Felix if he knew what had happened to Zephyr when the ice-cream van suddenly dinged out. All three looked up.

"Want one?" offered Felix. "There's time before my next class. I've entered the novice jumping—I always was a glutton for punishment!"

Minutes later they had found a shady spot beneath a spreading beech and were sampling giant cornets, speared with chocolate flake and coated with raspberry sauce.

"Grrreat!" Annis's tongue curled satisfyingly round the edge of her cone. Tiffin dozed, his rosettes fluttering on his bridle, but Cobber took a hungry look at Nicky's ice-cream and made a lunge for it.

"Oh no you don't!" Nicky scolded, dipping her finger and offering a lick. "There, that's your ration. The rest's mine!

Cobber scoffed it greedily and Felix laughed. "That's Pru's old Dandy, isn't it?"

Nicky nodded. "But I call him Cobber."

"Since when?" blurted Annis.

"Since now. I never did like the name Comet." Nicky glanced at Felix. "S'pose you've heard about him?"

"You bet! Pru and Pop's engagement party turned out a double celebration. Pru could spout about nothing else!"

Annis caught Nicky's eye. She said to Felix, "We noticed the ring. Do you mi. . . er, are you pleased?" Her cheeks went pink.

"Sure am! Pru's a good sort," Felix replied eagerly.

"She and Pop have a lot in common. He's bringing his thoroughbreds over from Ireland. Some are to be stabled at the Manor."

Both girls stood transfixed, ices half-way to their mouths.

"They're making gallops on the meadows," Felix went on blithely. "It"ll be great to watch. . . Uh, did I say something?" He paused uncertainly, his eyes puzzled.

Stunned into silence, Nicky and Annis could only stand and stare. Cobber, grabbing his chance, snatched Nicky's ice-cream and devoured it without her even noticing.

Annis found her voice. "You mean. . . the plan to build a leisure park has been scotched?"

Felix was nonplussed. "A leisure park?" he repeated. "At Chantley? You sure gotta be joking! What makes you think Pop'd do a dumb thing like that?"

"Some. . . something was said about a scheme," stammered Annis. And then. . . and then. . . "

An understanding look crossed Felix's face. "Guess things have got a bit twisted." He laughed. "Some time back Pop applied for a heliport on the meadow. I guess someone's got wind of it and sorta. . . elaborated!"

"A. . . a heliport?" Nicky gasped. "Are you sure?"

"Sure I'm sure! Pop does a lot of motorway driving. He thought a chopper would take some of the aggro out of travelling."

"Trust Chantley to get it wrong!" Annis said in a small voice. She frowned. "When is this heliport thing to be built?"

Felix finished his ice-cream and remounted the grey. "It isn't! The plans were turned down flat! Pop's had to resign himself to driving everywhere, I guess!" Gathering his reins, he gave a friendly nod and rode off to his next class.

The two girls watched him go. Annis hurriedly licked her ice-cream, which was melting in creamy runnels down her hand. Nicky turned on her in glee. "Well! What do you make of that?"

"I can't take it in!" Annis said shakily. "Wow, what a day this has been for surprises! Dad'll be gobsmacked, so will the rest of the village. . ."

Excitedly they began listing the people most likely to be affected by the news. When they came to the Shones Nicky's throat tightened. How she wished she had not fallen out with Zak. If only he had shown up to watch the mounted games. He would have been so proud of Cobber. Also, now that the truth—or at least, part of it—was out about Cobber, Nicky felt that he owed her an explanation.

Marcia too, was conspicuous by her absence. Nicky was sure that there had been mention of a Green stall.

The rest of the day slipped by. Nicky's parents were hustled off to the bar by the DC with Pru and Nigel for a celebratory drink. Nicky wondered if Tom had dared to g through with his mouse prank, but no screams emitted from the tent. Annis doubted there had been a mouse at all.

The girls watched the showjumping and made their plans. Now the PPP was definite, Nicky planned to approach her mother about turning one of their paddocks into a manege. It would be useful for all team members, but especially for Annis, who was constantly hampered by the Tinies.

The slow August dusk was drawing down as Nicky said goodbye to Annis and the Reeds and mounted Cobber. The parking area was emptying rapidly, the cars and trailers and wagons bumping and lurching over the uneven ground. Small pinpoints of lights could be seen all along the lane, as homebound traffic converged upon Chantley village. To avoid the lumbering vehicles, Nicky swung Cobber across the littered showground, with its smell of horses and bruised summer grass, and took the path through the forest.

Won. . .der. . .ful. . . day, Cobber's hooves seemed to beat out as he made his patient way along the deep-shadowed trail. Nicky leaned over and patted the warm skewbald neck, and a great gladness and contentment grew inside her. She had proved to Mum that she could ride. The PPP was on. Cobber was COBBER—she no longer had to remember to call him by a totally unsuitable name.

Best of all, Chantley was free from threat.

A sigh of pure happiness escaped her lips, and instead of keeping to the trail, she swung Cobber on to the track made rutted by the wheels of Zak's flatcart. She just HAD to share her joy with Marcia. She was eager to see Zak as well.

FOURTEEN

The yard at Keeper's Lodge was strangely deserted. Marcia must have bedded down the animals early, was Nicky's first thought as she rode between the empty pens and closed sheds. Houdini had failed to bark, and Nicky was quite relieved to see light spilling from the lodge window. At least someone was in.

Stiffly, she dismounted and hustled Cobber into the nearest empty shed. Securing the door, she paused and frowned across at the violet bulk of the stable block. That also was shuttered and quiet. No whinnying. No restless stamp of hoof. No Zak, whistling through his teeth as he groomed.

A plaintive yowling raked the silence. It issued from the smallest cat cabin, which had been empty since the tabby's kittens had gone. The sound came again, a primitive wail that made Nicky's flesh creep, and she turned at once for the house, quickening her step over the uneven cobblestones.

Something was missing from the hotch-potch yard but, with everything deep in shadow, she was at a loss to think what it was. She could hear the hound now, whining. She rapped sharply on the back door, pushed it open and entered the lodge. Houdini was at her side instantly, bestowing sloppy licks and waving his tail. Nicky bent to fuss him.

Marcia was seated in her chair beside the fire, her hands still for once. She looked up and greeted Nicky abstractedly.

"I expected you at the show with a Green stall," Nicky began, tipping papers from a chair and sitting down. "So did a lot of other people. Where were you?"

"Too busy!" was Marcia's excuse. She stood up and reached for the kettle.

"Oh Marcia, we've all had such an ACE time!" Still pervaded with that marvellous feeling of contentment and well-being, Nicky started to pour out the events of the day.

Marcia was slowly spooning tea into one of her new-design teapots. She said vaguely,, "Got a lovely white kitten out there, Nicky. Been neglected something shocking, but once I got it sorted, I thought as mebbe your ma might fancy it as a pet?"

Nicky, who had been half-way through relating her success with Cobber, stared blankly. "But. . . but Marcia," she stammered, "you know Mum HATES cats."

Marcia sniffed. "She won't hate this one. You'd like a fluffy white cat yourself, eh Nicky?"

Beset by the curious notion that Marcia was hedging, Nicky met her look squarely. "Of course, I'd love it. I'll have a word with Dad. He likes cats a lot. Between us we might be able to persuade Mum. . . But Marcia, I really came to see Zak."

Marcia's face fell and she began to make an unnecessary clatter with milk jug and mugs. "'Fraid then, Nicky," she muttered, "you're going to be disappointed."

Nicky's mind flew into turmoil. At once she realized what had been missing from the yard. It was Zak's flat-cart.

"He's gone, hasn't he?"

Marcia nodded, and abandoning the tea she dropped dispiritedly back into the chair. Houdini plonked himself at her feet and gazed at her with mournful amber eyes. "Been selling off his 'osses slowly. Sent his gear an' cart to the auction," Marcia declared sorrowfully. "It's sort o' quiet, without Zak. I keep expecting him to come in, whistling like."

"When did he leave?" Nicky asked in a small voice.

"Only a bit back. You've just missed him."

A lump came into Nicky's throat. She pictured Zak's slight eager figure, intent with his horses, and recalled the magical way they calmed to his touch. She hoped that a little magic had rubbed off on her. Pru might have established a few riding skills, but it had been Zak who had installed horse sense into her during those jogs along the leafy trails. He had also opened her eyes to Chantley; not the village, but the secret places, the forest and meadow and heath.

Now he was gone.

"But. . . but there was no need," Nicky stuttered. "That's what I came to say. The leisure park scare was all a mistake." Shakily she related what Felix had told them.

As she spoke, a knowing smile sneaked on to Marcia's face. Her eyes gleamed, a clear lapis blue; the sort of eyes that looked upon some invisible distance.

Nicky's explanation tailed away. "You knew, didn't you?" she said, quietly. "I didn't need to tell you. You knew all along."

Marcia gave a little crow of laughter. "Let's say I suspected. Stood to reason the man wouldn't want to live on top of his work. Besides. . ." her chin lifted and her voice grew certain ". . .I reckon it weren't part of the pattern."

There she goes again, thought Nicky. Talking in riddles!

Houdini uttered a troubled whimper. He was missing Zak already. Nicky reached out and stroked his head. "You'll miss Zak too, won't you Marcia?" she said.

Marcia gave a very audible sniff. "I s'pose he had to make his own way sometime, an' I've still got me rescue animals," she pointed out bravely. "And after your ma's bit o' good news today, I still got me little job at the school. Got to look on the bright side, ain't you, Nicky?"

Nicky said yes, but her mind was reeling. Typical of Zak to go skiving off, just when he thought the going was getting rough. He must have heard about Cobber and panicked. There might have been one or two other shady deals, too. And whatever had happened to Comet?

"You say ALL the horses are sold?" Nicky asked sharply. "Even the chestnut. . . I mean the bay?"

Marcia raised her thin shoulders in a shrug. "Bless you, I never did know if I was on me head or me heels with Zak's 'osses. Couldn't tell one from another, an' that's a fact! Between you an' me. . ." her voice hushed confidingly and she leaned forward, "I reckon our Zak learnt a trick or two off his da, regarding 'osses! I dunno, but some of 'em seemed to change mightily once they'd been here a bit, if you know what I mean?"

Her eyes challenged. Nicky said she understood perfectly.

"O' course," Marcia finished in a rush, "I never asked no questions. The 'oss dealing were Zak's business."

"But Marcia," Nicky cried. "Wherever has he gone to?"

"Why, he's bin accepted at a racing stable near Worcester." Marcia inclined her head proudly. "Zak's all set to be a jockey! I told you his deafness don't hold him back. He's left me a tidy sum from the sale of those 'osses, so I can get meself a tele. Got to watch him ride in them winners, ain't I?"

"Oh Marcia!" Nicky did not quite know what to say.

"He's took that there picture you painted him," Marcia said. "Said it were his favourite 'oss, and that being a bright girl you'd understand.

Nicky understood only too well. She had no doubt now that Zak was responsible for Cobber's theft, all those years ago. She pictured the young gypsy boy in his silent world, deserted by his father and throwing the blame on to the Parks-Harrisons. It would have been easy for him to sneak vengefully into Chantley's paddock in the dead of night, and steal away the skewbald. A skilful hour or two with stain and rasp, and the ageing Dandy was transformed into youthful Cobber!

Cobber though, had struck a soft spot and Zak, instead of selling the pony, had kept him. Then she had come gullibly along on Comet, and Zak had been unable to resist the temptation of a deal.

Everything slid into place. Zak's eagerness for her to

attend the rallies, his reluctance to show his own face—and no wonder he had laughed himself silly at the idea of Pru, unwittingly instructing a novice gymkhana enthusiast on Chantley's brilliant old Dandy!

Zak has made fools of all of us, Nicky thought furiously as she rose to leave. She was so outraged that Marcia's parting words barely registered. "Zak also said to tell you as your riding's improved no end, and to wish you luck with them games. And he give one of his laughs, you know, that could be funny or not?"

It was dark when Nicky left the forest. Cobber's hooves stirred a pungent smell of damp earth and leaf-mould. There was no moon, but the night was starlit. The little pipistrelle bats were out, flitting in shadowy clouds. A fox padded across the path. Beneath them, the badgers stirred in their sleepy tunnels.

"Come on," Nicky said, nudging Cobber with her heels, "time we were home."

Light blazed from the leaded windows of The Briars. Someone had switched on the yard and stable lamps too, Nicky noticed gladly. Anticipating his stable and supper, Cobber's pace quickened up the gravelled drive. Nicky was startled when her mother's voice rang out, and was surprised to see her emerge from the stable. "There you are at last! I was beginning to wonder if we should get up a search party."

"I called at Marcia's," Nicky replied. "Mum, did you know about the leis—"

"Yes yes. Pru told us, all a silly misunderstanding!" Mum waved a dismissive hand. She had a glow of excitement about her. "I've done um. . . Cobber's stable and left feed, hay and water."

"Oh lovely, thanks." Nicky was puzzled. She slid down, only to have the reins jerked from her grasp. She stood in disbelief as her mother led Cobber into his loose-box, whipped off his saddle and bridle and swept a brush over him.

"That'll do for now," Mum said, watching Cobber nose his manger and inspect his feed. She patted his solid rump. "He did well today, against those young ponies."

A little shiver slid down Nicky's spine. She did not care for the way her mother was looking at her, as if she had something of outstanding importance to relate. Nor did she take to being hustled towards the end loose-box, which lay in darkness.

From it emitted a shrill, distinct whinny. A hoof scraped the concrete, there was a swish of straw. Nicky's stomach contracted. Mum threw open the top-door. switched on the light. . . and there, blinking under the sudden beam, stood Zaks little bay!

Nicky stared at him in horror.

"I thought you'd be pleased!" Mum said delightedly. "I bought him from Zak Shone. I suppose Marcia told you he's sold his stable? Zephyr was the last to go. Zak admitted to keeping him until the right home came along!"

Nicky was instantly suspicious. She turned on her mother accusingly. "When did this pony arrive?"

Mum flinched as if she had been struck."What? Well, this evening of course. I took some jumble up to Marcia's house early today, before we went to the show. Zak was schooling Zephyr in their field. He rode over and we got talking. He is an oddity, but he DOES know about his horses. He assured me that Zephyr was the next step up for you. Oh dear, Nicky, I must say you don't seem very thrilled!" Her voice throbbed with disappointment.

The bay came over to them with purposeful strides and put his head enquiringly over the half-door.

You dare bite! Nicky challenged him silently. His brown head lifted askance, his eyes glinting, his top lip giving a little curl—Comet might almost have been laughing. He did not nip, but instead reached out and gently lipped Nicky's sleeve for titbits. Numbly she searched her pocket, found a polo and offered it.

"Zak'd say this was spoiling him," she mumbled as Comet accepted the treat and crunched it up.

"Would he?" Her mother took an anxious step closer. "You are pleased, aren't you, Nicky? Zak assured me Zephyr will make a gymkhana pony. He's super-fast and can turn on a coin. He's a quick learner—"

"But Mum," Nicky burst out. "Thanks and everything, but I'm perfectly happy with Cobber."

"I know you are," came the soothing reply. "Cobber's a schoolmaster and exactly right for you, but you've got to accept that he's an old pony and might have to be retired, for his own sake. Oh, don't look so alarmed, we'll keep him always. Promise."

Nicky heaved a sigh.

Mum put a gentle hand on her shoulder. "Listen, I haven't gone into this without a great deal of thought. Pru has seen Zephyr. She likes him and has offered to help school him. She wondered if I'd allow Mo Stephens, whose Shetland is not really suitable, to ride him initially. I don't mind at all but of course, the final decision rests with you. Zephyr's your pony."

Her hand fell away and went worriedly to her face. Nicky looked again at the bay. Maybe this was meant. All part of some intrinsic pattern. Marcia's pattern.

Nicky glanced thoughtfully at her mother. "That'll be fine. I felt sorry for Mo today. She's so keen and though Dinah Mite's good, she'll never be Wembley standard."

Mum smiled. "Then that's settled. DO show a bit of enthusiasm to your father, love," she warned, casting the study window a furtive glance. "He's forked out a lot of money for Zephyr."

Over a thousand, Nicky recalled. Was there no end to Zak's cunning?

"Now," Mum said briskly. "I promised Dad a special supper to round off the day, so I'll leave you and Zephyr to get to know each other and make a start." She raised a hopeful brow and left.

Nicky stood a moment, frowning at the pony. Bracing herself, she opened the stable door and went inside. Instantly Comet was there, nuzzling her pockets, scouting for more titbits. Nicky pushed his nose away and stroked his glossy bay neck. Comet did not nip, nor did he lift a threatening hoof. Zak had taught him well.

He had also had the last laugh, Nicky thought wryly. She fancied she could hear him, chuckling across the night-time spaces to where she stood.

Marcia's pattern was complete.

Moving to the door, she looked into the starlit night which still echoed to the sound of Zak's laughter, and winged a silent message back to him.

'Good fortune, Zak, and checkmate, because when Mo Stephens manages to acquire a gymkhana pony of her own I intend to ride Zephyr. Until then, I'll stick with your Cobber.'

And then her peace was shattered. Whatever would she do when the brown and black stain wore off, and Zephyr became a bright, oh-so-familiar chestnut?